C000115489

Small Deaths

Small Deaths

by

S. W. Williams

All the characters in this novel (apart, of course, from Edmond Locard) are fictitious and any resemblance to real persons, living or dead, is purely coincidental. The places and events are mostly historically and geographically accurate; some are fictitious. The reader can decide which is which.

SMALL DEATHS © S.W. Williams
ISBN 978-1-9996652-2-4
eISBN 978-1-9996652-3-1
Published in 2017 by Crime Scene Books

The right of S.W. Williams to be identified as the author of this work has been asserted by her in accordance with the Copyright, Designs and Patents Act 1988.

Maps by MapArt.co.uk
Book design by Clockwork Graphic Design
Cover design George Foster Covers
Printed and bound in Great Britain by Marston Book Services Ltd, Oxfordshire

Dedication

In memory of Muriel Rose

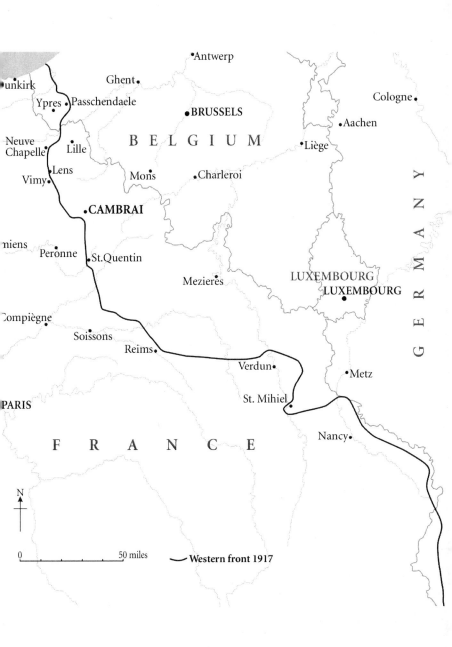

•Antwerp

Ghent•

unkirk

Ypres• •Passchendaele

•BRUSSELS

Cologne•

Neuve
Chapelle•

•Lille

B E L G I U M

•Aachen

•Liège

Lens•

Vimy•

Mons•

•Charleroi

•CAMBRAI

niens

Peronne•

•St.Quentin

•Mezieres

LUXEMBOURG

LUXEMBOURG•

Compiègne•

Soissons•

Reims•

•Verdun

•Metz

St. Mihiel•

PARIS

Nancy•

F   R   A   N   C   E

G   E   R   M   A   N   Y

N
↑

0   50 miles   ⌒ **Western front 1917**

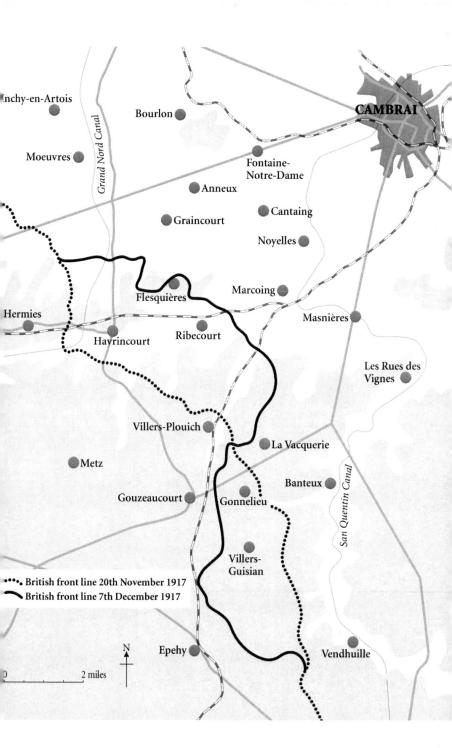

nchy-en-Artois

Grand Nord Canal

Bourlon

Moeuvres

CAMBRAI

Fontaine-
Notre-Dame

Anneux

Graincourt

Cantaing

Noyelles

Flesquières

Marcoing

Hermies

Masnières

Ribecourt

Havrincourt

Les Rues des
Vignes

Villers-Plouich

La Vacquerie

Metz

San Quentin Canal

Banteux

Gouzeaucourt

Gonnelieu

Villers-
Guisian

•••• British front line 20th November 1917
⎯ British front line 7th December 1917

N

0   2 miles

Epehy

Vendhuille

Mystery graves in wartime woods

The Commonwealth War Graves Commission, in their ongoing task of finding and recovering remains of British and Commonwealth soldiers killed in both world wars, has announced the discovery of eight graves in a wood not far from Cambrai in northern France. The scene of intense fighting during the summer and autumn of 1917, the area is known to harbour untold numbers of unidentified soldiers killed in the conflict. The woods where the remains were found have long been the subject of local folklore as the resting place of a number of dead from World War I, but it was only in the last few weeks that forensic anthropologists began their excavation of the site. They have reported that the remains discovered appear not to be those of soldiers, but rather of a number of small children. Investigations continue.

www.theglobalguardian.com/world

July 2017

1917

CHAPTER 1

1st November, morning

The boy was playing at the edge of the stream, poking at the water with a stick, half pretending to fish, half wanting the fish to play with him. He didn't notice when the shadow fell over him. Hands lifted him almost gently, one covering his mouth in case a cry escaped, and then child and man were gone together into the shadows of the wood.

The man carried him carefully but firmly, like a squirming lamb needing to be weaned from its mother, he thought. Yes, that was it, a lamb to be sheltered. He hurried through the woods to his special place. A rough lean-to of branches and sticks, a clearing with blackened stones where he had had a fire the previous winter. 'You'll be safe here, Little Lamb,' he said. 'You'll be safe here.'

***

Jack leaned against the slight warmth of the brickwork, and simply shut his eyes. The sun seeped through his skin and soothed his aching shoulders, his heavy-beyond-bearing limbs.

He was almost without thought, stupefied with weariness. He had been driving and lifting, carrying and comforting, for forty-eight hours now, catching a few brief moments of rest, here and there, stunned islands of numbness in the buffeting storm of noise and wild movement.

The worst, for the moment, was over, and he had simply walked off the ward and out behind the barn and stables which were serving as the Casualty Clearing Station. Now he stood, ears ringing, eyes able at last to close, his mind clenched tight against all he'd seen.

With infinite tiredness he half raised his eyelids and fumbled in his breast pocket for his precious packet of Woodbines. Something inside him smiled as he imagined Dr Werner's despairing tirade, 'Ach, Johann, you must not the cigarettes be smoking. Your lungs, they cannot work with smoke in them.' It was true, his breathing was dreadful every time he lit up, but it hardly seemed to matter, and he couldn't conceive of a day, an hour passing without the fragile comfort of a smoke.

The woman glanced across the farmyard to the stable building. No horses now. They were long gone. Just men, wounded, dying, laid out in twos and threes where the stalls had been. And their carers, moving between them, sleeping in heaps in the straw of the loft, or standing, like this one now, dazed in the sunlight, his face raised towards the thin winter warmth.

She gave herself a shake. No point crying over spilt milk, or lost horses. There was enough to do, simply cobbling together the bits of a life that were left. She glanced up at the sun – almost midday. Another couple of hours and she would need to fetch Alex from her mother's. She turned back into the house. The beds and the dishes and the food – such as it was – would not do themselves.

Jack saw her go out of the corner of his eye. He turned his head just enough to watch her as she went back into the farmhouse where half a dozen of the officers were billeted when they were out of the line. A bed, Jack mused, when was the last time he had stretched out and slept between clean sheets, with nothing but darkness and silence?

***

Major John Carter RAMC paused in something like wonder when he got out of the car which had fetched him up from the CCS. Every person and animal and vehicle around him seemed to be moving with purposeful energy. The very air appeared to hum and quiver with anticipation.

'Well,' he said to himself, straightening his uniform and striding towards the main building housing Divisional HQ. 'Watson old chap, without a doubt, the game is afoot.' A light smile played briefly over his face as he recalled the zest and brilliance of his favourite fictional character. 'If only they could hand this whole bally mess over to Holmes and Mycroft. They'd have it sorted in no time.'

Snapping out of his reverie when he reached the guard at the door, he returned the soldier's salute and enquired where the medics' briefing was being held.

'Up the main stairs, right at the top, second door along the corridor on the left, sir.'

'Thank you, private,' replied the major crisply.

He stepped into the gloomy, rather chilly building and made his way up the stairs.

On reaching the meeting room, he saw it was set up for a significant briefing. Forty or fifty chairs were laid out in rows, facing a long table with half a dozen more chairs behind it. On the far wall, facing the rows of chairs, a large map had been pinned up. At the moment it was covered by a sheet. Doubtless, when the time was right, all would be revealed.

***

The major's briefing had been brisk, workmanlike, exciting and terrifying in equal measure. Sitting in the back of the car being driven back to the CCS, he started to go through his notes, beginning to put in order of priority everything that needed to be done in readiness for the forthcoming battle. There were a number of difficulties he could foresee, not the least of them being the requirement to keep all the preparations as secret as possible, surprise being, as they had been told forcefully a number of times, absolutely of the essence. Fundamentally, as far as he and his men were concerned, it came down to three essentials - supplies topped up, beds emptied, and everyone in position and ready to jump to it when the time came. The Powers That Be had seemed positively optimistic over this new plan of attack. The major wished he could believe in his superiors as much as they appeared to believe in themselves.

Back at the CCS, he dismissed the car and driver, and made his way over to the bedroom in the farmhouse which also served as his private office. He had a lot of planning to do.

***

In the silence of his home, isolated right at the edge of the village, the man sat at the ancient wooden table, his hands resting quietly round the slender bottle still half full of beer. It had taken a long time, the best part of two years, in fact, but he had thought, and watched, questioned and observed, and now he had it all set in his mind. Ten. Ten to start with. He told over their names, more precious to him than any prayer. These he would rescue. These he would save. The first was already safe.

***

Jack had already spent three years in a sanatorium in the German Alps when it became clear that war was imminent. There was no question of his becoming a soldier, even if he had felt he wanted to, needed to, should. His lungs were riddled with TB and he could barely walk fifty yards without having to rest his head against a wall, a tree, whatever was to hand, and quiet his heaving chest. He was already, he had smiled equivocally to himself, one of the walking wounded.

The doctors had become very distressed when it was known that their English patients could no longer stay with them in the clear mountain air. Jack and the others, some fifteen of them, had been wrapped and tucked into the stiff, scratchy seats of the little Alpine railway, and had found themselves ticking their way down from the mountains, across Germany, across Belgium, into France and onto one of the last ferries to leave Calais in that early August.

He had gone up on deck and watched the water dancing in the brilliant sunshine. The French coastline dropped away, and, almost immediately, the English coastline rose up ahead. It had been five years since Jack had been back in England, first in Paris and then in the sanatorium. He had no idea what he would do, where he would go, how he would feel. England, he thought, held nothing for him. It was going to be a strange time.

And it had been, stranger than he could ever have dreamed. War was declared and crowds cheered and waved flags. Young men, boys, queued from dawn to dusk to join the army and 'go and do their bit'. Jack could not credit it. Did they not understand what war was like? Did they not understand what high explosives could do to the fragile human frame? Had they learned nothing from the war in South Africa?

Jack had been a reporter for a few months in South Africa twelve years before, at the end of the war against the Boers. He'd seen the aftermath of fighting, he'd seen the concentration camps, the desperate, hungry children, the despairing, bitter women. He had written as fully and vehemently as he could against the mad inhumanity of it all, the inglorious greed for gold and diamonds and land. And he had been recalled.

'We mustn't upset the good burghers of Croydon over their tea and toast, must we, Jack?' said the editor, not unkindly, but with a firm cynicism born of years with the newspaper. 'But you do write well, you infernal little cur,' he smiled at Jack. 'If you don't like war, let's see how you do with art.' And so Jack had been despatched to Paris, to become the newspaper's art correspondent. And he had loved it. He'd met all sorts of interesting men, and some fascinating women. Some extraordinarily difficult women too. He had sat in bars until the small hours, sipping carefully on a glass of absinthe – he wanted to be one of them in some ways, but not in the ways that led to desperate feelings and desperate actions. Ironic, as it turned out. He'd guarded his health so carefully. Not sleeping with the women, or men, who offered themselves to him. Not drinking ruinously. Not taking the drugs which were always readily on offer for those who knew what to ask for, and of whom. But still he'd fallen ill, and found himself becoming the classic type of the romantic artist his companions so much despised. He'd lie in his small room, right at the top of the narrow building (not quite an attic, but close enough) and cough and cough into his handkerchief, shivering, feverish, white with illness and exhaustion, the cloth crumpled and foul with his blood. In the end it had taken the ever-reliable Evelyn coming over from England, worried at the lack of letters, and bustling around, taking him in hand as only an elder sister could do. Just as well she'd not married. Ever since Mother's death, he and Father had completely depended upon her to make things right when they went wrong, and to keep things running smoothly no matter what.

Evelyn had contacted the Embassy, got from them the name of a doctor 'who we can trust' and quickly established that Jack had TB. Which he had known, of course, but hadn't wanted to think about. He was tired, and cross, and very afraid. Evelyn shook him, literally as well as metaphorically, into some sort of shape. She got him out of bed and had him out in the fresh air from dawn till dusk. She bought litres of cow's milk from the local dairy, and forced him to drink glass after glass every day. She fed him on wholesome foods and vegetables, scoured with energy from the local markets. Nothing seemed to make much difference though. Jack continued to get thinner and paler, his eyes more hectic, the handkerchiefs still soaked with gleaming fresh blood every time he coughed – and he was soon coughing almost continuously.

Evelyn went back to the doctor. What could he suggest? Clear mountain air, he replied. Which mountains, where? The Germans, he had heard, had an excellent sanatorium on the shores of Lake Constance. Perhaps they could try there?

Evelyn returned to the Embassy and had them, first, find out about the sanatorium and then book Jack in for an extended stay under the care of the head of the Clinic, Dr Jakob Werner. She had taken him there herself, looking after him firmly and fussily on the long train journey, as he lay slumped on the seat, coughing, moaning, sweating.

The sanatorium was large and modern, with wide sweeps of balconies overlooking the deep blue waters of Lake Constance, with the crisp, snow-clad mountains beyond. The regime was simple, Spartan and effective. All day the patients lay in rows on wooden deckchairs (like chrysalises, Jack had thought), wrapped in heavy blankets, only their white faces showing over the top of the wrappings, with woollen caps on their heads and pulled down over their ears. Sometimes they chatted in a desultory manner, picking their way through fragments of language from French to German to Polish to English to Russian to Italian and beyond. Most often, though, they sat in silence, gazing out numbly at the deep blue, icy water, feeling as little as possible. Nurses moved amongst them with quiet solicitation, bringing them hot drinks at intervals – strange herbal concoctions that tasted of grass and bitter things, which filled their mouths with unexpected aftertastes for hours to come. Gradually, gradually, some of them moved out of their torpor, and began to walk a little, lift their eyes a little, from lake to mountain, and to take some interest in the world around them, as though, after all, they might have a future.

It was two months before Jack felt able to read anything. At first it was only old familiar books, Trollope and Dickens mostly, friends he could rely on, then, gradually, after more time had passed, more alchemical potions had been swallowed, more strolls taken around the perimeter of the verandah, and even, on a couple of occasions, into the edges of the grounds, Jack found himself picking up newspapers and scanning the pages.

The sanatorium had newspapers in all the European languages. At first, Jack stuck to the arts pages, particularly in the French papers, reading a few sentences here and there about the people he had met in Paris, the exhibitions they were mounting, the scandal they were causing, the excitement they were stirring up. It seemed an odd, irrel-

21

evant world to him now. What on earth did it matter whether a woman was painted soft or angular, whether paint was applied in sweeps or stipples or dollops? How could he once have cared? He would lay down the newspaper, and simply sit back on his deckchair, draw up the blanket, and shut his eyes. The silence, the cold, his breath slightly warm against his lips, that was all that was real to him now.

Then, slowly, again very slowly, Jack started noticing the headlines in the papers, the news articles, the political commentaries. It seemed that everyone was getting very exercised about an assassination in Austro-Hungary. A crown prince and his morganatic wife – what a wonderful word, morganatic, and what an extraordinary concept. It appeared, Jack gleaned from articles in French and English and German, that there might be a war in Europe. He wondered what that meant, and whether it meant anything for him. If there were a war between the English and the German Empires, would that affect them, the chrysalises, high up here in the mountains, with their smiling, solicitous nurses?

He soon learned. Dr Werner brought them all together in the main hall of the sanatorium, men sitting, some slumped, in rows of hard chairs, the nurses and other staff ranged standing around the back and along the sides. All foreign nationals had to leave the sanatorium within the month, could they please make arrangements with their families, the sanatorium would be running buses to the train station every day for the next seven days.

Jack went back to his narrow room and wrote a letter to Evelyn. A week later, his small suitcase packed, a bundle of books tied tightly with string on the seat beside him, Jack was on the train. A small train first of all, down the mountainside, then a larger, much busier train, full of slightly frightened, slightly excited people, heading for the Belgian coast. Then the boat from Ostend, crammed now with people carrying bundles, silent, fearful. Jack found a corner of the first class saloon where he could sit down on the floor in a corner of the bar. He leaned back against the polished mahogany and watched the huddled clumps of families around him. Some of them were straining to see out of the window towards the Belgian coast as it disappeared behind them, some were craning forward to try and catch their glimpse of the cliffs of England, most though had their heads down, thinking of what they had had to abandon, wondering what they were going to find ahead.

Jack wasn't thinking at all. He still carried with him the calm and detachment of the sanatorium. He felt that this world of worried men and women had nothing to do with him. He had not sought this war, he did not know what it was about or what it meant. All he wanted was to go home. Slowly, though, as he sat with his back against the warm wood, a thought took shape. He realised he had no home. He was just the same as all these other wretched, uprooted, unhappy people. How surprising. He tried the idea on, holding it up against his picture of himself. He couldn't make it fit. Shrugging slightly, he settled back again into his customary torpor. He would go and stay with Evelyn. She'd sort it out. She'd sort him out. She always did.

CHAPTER 2

1st November, afternoon - 2nd November, overnight and early morning

Murray lay sprawled on the fire step. The Boy Jones (to distinguish him from the Man Jones) stood above him, crouched, looking through the periscope across to the Jerries half a mile away. Murray tried to angle himself so that the midday sun touched his face. They'd been in the line for coming up to ten days – another four and they'd be relieved, squirming back down the supply lines to the road, and then tumbling down the road to the rear, to fresh water, thin wine (if he could scrounge some up) and sleep.

The guns were thumping further down the line – some other poor buggers would be going over the top then, he supposed. He found his eyes shutting, but forced them open. Murray was determined to feel the sun, to see the day. He wriggled round and knelt up on the fire step next to Boy. Slowly, slowly, he reached up so that his fingers were on the top step, and then he drew himself up by inches, his face close to the caked, dry mud of the trench wall, and lifted his head so that he could see across No Man's Land.

Murray rested his gaze on the clumps of grass which lay lank, ungrazed, across the open space. In the summer there had been flowers – poppies, daisies, something low and blue he couldn't name, thronging the ground. They had thrived on last winter's dead, unrecovered. Now they too were dead, but next year they would bloom again. Oh for crying out loud! Tired metaphors for tired minds. Murray shook his head in self-disgust. He laid his cheek against the cold trench wall and shut his eyes.

He dozed, dreaming of summer grass.

'Where are you off to? Wait for me?' He turns to see Miranda's slight figure come skittering down the steps and into the garden. She hurls herself along the path after him.

'You can't come. I'm going fishing. You'll frighten the fish.'

'I won't, I promise I won't. I'll sit as still as, as still as...' The little girl comes to a halt, racking her brains, her foot tapping out her impatience on the path. 'As still as a gargoyle!' she cries out triumphantly. It is a word he'd taught her just a few days before, when they'd been coming back from church.

'Alright, then, Turnip Top,' he concedes, laying a hand on top of her head and ruffling her straight blond hair. 'But any wriggling and I'm packing you back off to Mrs Mifflin, understood?'

She grins, 'Understood,' and slips her small, slightly sticky hand into his.

It is he who tires of fishing first. The sun is too hot, the day is too languid, the grass along the riverbank is too soft and lush and inviting. The two of them lie belly down side by side in the long grass and gaze into the limpid waters. Weeds waver in the current, little fish dart, larger fish saunter through the shadowed depths. Together they drift into sleep in the hot sun.

Then Edwin's voice, calling from the end of the garden.

'Sir, sir, wake up, you'll have Jerry taking a pop at us if you don't get down.' Murray saw Boy Jones' face peering up at him anxiously, and felt his hand tugging at the hem of his tunic. He looked blearily around, caught between his dream and the reality of the trenches.

Slowly he slid down the fire steps, past the relieved Boy, and resumed his seat, half on the bottom step and half stretched out across the duckboards at the bottom of the trench. He shook his head, trying to free his mind from the echoes of Edwin's voice calling to him excitedly that war had been declared, trying to free his limbs from the memory of the warmth and wonderful comfort of that high summer.

With sleepy fingers he reached into his breast pocket and took out his notebook and a stub of pencil. He'd promised to write to Miranda every day. He was all she had left now that Edwin had been killed. Mother had retreated into some place where she couldn't be reached, the war didn't exist, and her greatest concern was that she couldn't get anybody to come in and cut the grass properly these days.

Dear Turnip Head, he wrote. *Nearly at the end of our holiday on the Côte de Boue. Not that it's too bouey at the moment. In fact, it's a lovely drowsy winter's day, almost like summer, just like that day in August '14 when we went fishing together. Remember that, Turnip? It seems a world away, not just 3 short years. And how much has changed! How you have changed! Not a tedious, sticky 9 year old any more, but a lady now, doing all sorts of useful things. I really loved the scarf, Turnip, and I'm sure all 7 feet will be really handy come the colder weather! And I love your letters. Keep them coming. That and the cake. Love and kisses, M.*

He tore the sheet from his notebook and crouched his way back into his dugout to find an envelope. With luck he might get the letter away with the messenger this evening, assuming he came. Then two days, three nights, and proper sleep.

Murray's father had been a village doctor, with a practice just outside Oxford in a little place called Eynsham. They'd had a biggish house a little outside the village – only the squire and the vicar had bigger ones – with a garden that ran down to a path and then to the river beyond. After Father died, Mother and the three children had stayed on in the big house, although it was really too large for them. Mother didn't quite know how to cope, and sank into a gloomy listlessness, not dragging herself out of bed until 10 or 11 in the mornings, and then spending most of the day on the chaise longue in the conservatory. Sometimes she went visiting to the other ladies in the village, sometimes they came and visited her, but as a rule she governed the little household languidly, from a supine position.

The two boys and Miranda were educated in a haphazard way, with a series of tutors and governesses. Mrs Coverdale didn't want the children away from her, but, on the other hand, she didn't want them disturbing her. So long as they were polite and clean, and appeared to be able to read and write and play a few small tunes on the piano, Mrs Coverdale was satisfied that her duty as a mother was being done.

The result was that the children spent a lot of their time together, playing inside the house or out, depending on the weather. They were more than just brothers and sister. They were all the society any of them had, and they grew into a close band, devoted to each other, and fiercely antagonistic to anyone who sought to come between them. A number of tutors and one particularly tiresome governess had been driven to give in their notice through a sustained campaign of disdain and disobedience from the children when the educators had rashly sought to teach them separately and to ration the time the children spent together.

Inevitably, though, time passed, and the children grew into different people, with different interests.

Edwin, as the eldest, was the first to feel the pull of the world beyond, and especially of Mary Smith, the vicar's eldest daughter. He spent, it seemed to Murray and Miranda, an incomprehensible amount of time going to church, helping at church, and even volunteering to assist Mary in the Sunday School. But Edwin's absence only drew the two younger children together, with Miranda tagging along behind or, if permitted, beside Murray as he explored the countryside around their home. Together they fished, or sat in the woods watching the fox cubs playing in the spring, or lying breathlessly in wait for the snuffling badgers going ponderously about their business as dusk set in.

Then came the War.

First Edwin went, volunteering on the day war was declared, only telling Mother when the deed was done, and leaving her even more prostrate, a handkerchief pressed to her mouth, her back pressed down into the cushions of the chaise as though she was trying to drown in them. Edwin kissed her perfunctorily on the brow, and rushed up the road to the village to break the news to Mary. It was a complicated moment, as Mary deeply disapproved of the war and of any kind of fighting, while at the same time deeply approving of Edwin, his flushed, enthusiastic face, and his courage.

Edwin left, and the household settled around his absence. Letters came, then Edwin himself, strange in a stiff uniform with creaking boots, and a servant who accompanied him home ('His family's too far for him to get back to, Mother. You don't mind him lodging with us here, do you?'). They had barely come than they were gone again, though now Mary wore a slender gold band with a single small diamond on her finger.

More letters, postcards, long silences, and then the telegram.

Murray and Miranda learnt the news through hearing their mother's cries. Rushing down from the schoolroom where they'd been playing canasta, they found their mother standing in the hallway, the telegram in her hand, her mouth open in a single, long, interminable scream.

Even when the new doctor, Doctor Green, had come and settled her into her bed and dosed her into unconsciousness with laudanum, the house seemed to echo with the wrenching sound of her grief. The children went out, and wandered aimlessly, anguished, uprooted, touching familiar trees, walls, gateways, trying to connect the world they knew to the world they had entered.

Two years passed. The war had settled into a routine horror, as father after father, brother after brother went from the village, some coming back on leave, some bandaged, limping, wounded, some not coming back at all.

Murray and Miranda talked together about what they should do. He was now seventeen, she was eleven, yet they seemed on an equal footing in understanding.

'You know I'll have to go, don't you,' said Murray one evening as they sat together in the parlour after dinner, gazing into the fire. It had been two years since their mother had last been downstairs. She lived in her room, the curtains drawn, barely speaking, leaving the running of the household to her children.

'I know,' said Miranda. 'I'm going to volunteer for the VAD as soon as I can. I look almost eighteen, don't I?'

Murray looked across at his slender, gawky sister, curled up in the leather armchair which had once been their father's. 'With a hat and some proper shoes, and a stiff serge suit, you could probably manage it today, so long as you wash the cinder toffee off your fingers,' he grinned. 'But seriously, Turnip Top, I can't not go. It seems so dreadfully unfair that other chaps should be having to go through it all, and I just sit here cosy and comfortable in front of a roaring fire with my best chum.' He paused, 'Could you manage, do you think, with Mother and everything?'

Miranda responded to the seriousness of his tone. 'Of course I can, M. I've been telling Mrs Mifflin what to do around the house for the last two years, and if I'm stuck I can ask Mrs Smith.'

The pair fell silent. After Edwin's death, Mary Smith had left the village, unable to stay in the place where she had been so happy, and where that happiness could never come again. She was nursing in France, as close to the line as she was allowed, and refusing all leave. She just wanted to be where the men were, tending to each of them as she had been unable to tend to the man she loved.

'Very well, then,' said Murray, resolute. 'I'll go in the morning. Don't tell Ma until after I've left.'

'I won't,' said Miranda, unfolding from the deep armchair and stepping over to her brother. She knelt at his feet in front of the fire and rested her head in his lap. 'I know you can't promise anything,' she said, her voice muffled against his leg, 'but can you try as hard as you possibly can to keep yourself safe? Don't volunteer for anything, will you? Albert said it's volunteering gets you killed.'

'I promise I won't volunteer, Turnip,' said Murray, resting his hand on his sister's head. 'I'll just go and do what I can, as well as I can, and keep my head down. You know better than anyone, I'm no hero.' He stroked her hair. 'I just want to do what I have to do, get home, and then get enough tutoring to get myself into Balliol to study law. It seems to me there's a distinct lack of order and reason in the world today, and it'll be up to you and me to supply it in the years to come.'

Miranda raised her head, and looked up into her brother's face. 'Well, that'll be a poor show for future ages, won't it?' They smiled at each other, trusting, open, at rest, perhaps for the last time living the life they knew, knowing that from this evening on, they would be parted, would see different sights, learn different things, become different people.

Miranda laid her head down again, and so they sat until the fire died down and the room began to chill, the almost man resting his hand on the head of the most precious being in his world, the hardly child resting her head on the knee of the only person she knew she could rely on.

Their courage lay cold on their shoulders when they finally rose and went to their separate beds.

***

The order had just come through. Another night patrol.

Murray shrugged. He was tired out, his men were exhausted, nothing had changed in their sector in weeks. Everyone knew where everyone was, everyone knew that no-one was going anywhere, so why a patrol? What on earth were they supposed to discover? That the Boches had smuggled elephants into the trenches and were going to charge over like Hannibal down from the Alps? Still, his not to reason why. Murray paused, and decided not to finish the quotation, not even silently, not even only in his head.

He went over to where the men were finishing their evening meal, huddled round the brazier. It wasn't really a cold night, but then it wasn't really physical warmth the men were seeking.

'We're up the line and over the top again tonight, boys,' Murray told them quietly. 'You, you, you and you,' he said, gesturing towards four of the more experienced men. 'Haines, Greenleaf, Finch, Sumpter, you are cordially invited to join me for tonight's entertainment.' The men nodded sombrely. 'And you, Jones, fancy a bit of fun?' The young man nodded eagerly. He'd go anywhere Lieutenant Coverdale asked him to go, to the gates of Hell and back if that's what the lieutenant wanted.

***

At two o'clock, the rum ration came round.

Soon after it was time for his small group to make their way, slithering through the slimy mud, over the top of the trench, through the gap in the wire and into No Man's Land.

Murray went first, his pistol gripped in damp fingers, a whistle uselessly dangling round his neck. Since the whole patrol had to be conducted in total silence, a whistle was as much use as a chocolate poker.

Murray waited the far side of the wire for his small, trembling band to form up, belly down, on either side of him. At his whispered command, they rose tentatively to a crouch and started to make their way, slowly, slowly, towards the enemy lines.

Every so often a flare would go up and hang with infinite slow brightness in the air. Each man would crouch and freeze, thinking as hard as he could, 'I am mud, I am earth, I am a tree stump,' as if his thoughts could divert the snipers' gaze.

Then the Verey light would sputter out and the night become black again. Murray touched the shoulders of the men on each side, who in turn touched the men beside them, until all were in contact again, and the small band would resume its painful grope towards the Boches.

It was when they were about three quarters of the way across that Boy Jones slipped and fell head first into a shell hole. The splash he made when he landed split the night, and suddenly everything erupted around them.

***

Murray huddled down into the mud, making himself as small as he could, as a machine gun raked over the earth in front, behind, beside them.

He heard one man cry out, but dared not raise or turn his head to see who it was or how badly he was hit. His thoughts froze to a single point, a single phrase, 'Make it stop, make it stop, make it stop.' And then it did. The silence was almost more unnerving than the gunfire. He knew what was happening. The Germans were waiting for them to move and begin to regroup, then they'd send up a Verey light and wipe out the lot of them.

With infinite care Murray unlaced his fingers from where, instinctively, irrationally, he had clamped them over the back of his neck when the machine gun had first opened up. Then, with the same inch-by-inch caution, he straightened his legs and turned his head, still flat against the mud, until he was looking to his left. Finch and Sumpter were lying flat down, their faces turned towards him. With the same slow, infinite caution, Murray moved an arm until his hand was close to his face and lifted a finger to his lips. Silence, he cautioned the men, and then, with a brief gesture, stay still, stay in place. Finch gave the smallest of nods and turned his head just enough to pass the message on to Sumpter. Murray waited just long enough to see Sumpter nod, then turned his head the other way. The view over there was less reassuring. Haines was the man wounded. Murray couldn't see where, he could just see the man's white face and the enormous effort he was making not to utter a sound. Haines had his upper lip clenched between his teeth and his eyes clamped shut. Murray needed to get him back to the lines as soon as he could. That much was clear. Beyond Haines, Greenleaf was curled down into a tiny dip in the mud. He was looking at Murray, waiting for orders. And then there was Jones. Murray couldn't see him – couldn't hear him either. He could guess, though. The water in the shell hole would be icy cold, and full of vile floating things, unpleasant things that swim, and really nasty things that had sunk to the bottom of the pool. And Jones was stuck in it.

It was probably only a second or two that Murray lay there, thinking of the order in which to proceed, and trying to work out how to get the small party back to the infinitely seductive safety of the trench behind them.

Just then, a Verey light floated up into the night air. The men all pressed their faces to the mud again – all except Haines, who simply lay locked into stillness by fear and pain. The machine gun opened up again, but it was clear by the way the gunner was strafing in a haphazard way that he couldn't see the men and was simply hoping for a lucky hit.

Murray was reassured. If the gunner couldn't see them while the star shell hovered over them, then there was a chance they might be able to get out of this alive.

As soon as the Verey light had sputtered and gone out, Murray wriggled silently over to Finch. Putting his mouth against the man's ear, he spoke so quietly it almost seemed as if he was sending the words directly from his mind into the mind of the man beside him.

'Haines is wounded. You three need to get him back to the lines. I'll fish out Jones and follow. Don't make a sound – they can't see us at the moment, but they bloody well can hear us.'

Finch nodded and reached out to touch Sumpter on the shoulder. Murray waited just long enough to see the message passed on and the two men make their way, belly down, towards Haines and Greenleaf, then he set off to make his own way, snakelike, to the shell hole.

It felt against all reason to be going towards the enemy lines, towards the bitter, spiteful machine gun, but he couldn't just leave Boy out there.

It took about ten minutes for Murray to get close enough to the shell hole to peer down over the edge into the pitch blackness below him. He lay, waiting for his eyes to adjust to this extra level of dark, and searching through the shadows for some sign of Jones. Then he saw him, almost directly below him, up to his waist in the slimy water, drenched and his face covered in mud. Only his eyes showed glimmering in the dark, wide with fear and trust. He was waiting, quietly, for Murray to save him.

Reaching down, he felt a wet hand reaching up. Quickly he gripped it. The skin came off in his clasp, sliding limp and cold between his fingers. Not Boy then. Murray clenched his teeth to stop himself retching and leant further over the edge of the shell hole.

He lifted out his arm so that Boy could see it and held his hands to his lips. He nodded towards the enemy lines. Boy nodded. He knew they were close. He knew they could be heard. Murray stretched out his hand towards Boy and made a waiting gesture. Boy nodded again. He seemed to have perfect faith that Murray had some sort of solution and would magic the both of them safe across the pitted, clinging mud to their own lines.

Murray had never before felt such a weight of trust on his shoulders. He wanted to shout to the child, 'I don't know what to do! I'm stuck here too! Why don't *you* help *me*?' But he didn't. Instead he slithered slightly backwards until he was below the lip of the shell hole and gradually unbuckled his sodden belt with stiff, reluctant fingers.

He unfastened his holster, and shoved it into the waist band of his trousers, then wrapped the tongue end of his belt around his hand. Snaking back to the shell hole, he reached down, with the belt dangling from his extended arm. Jones grasped at it with both hands. 'Slowly,' Murray mouthed. Jones nodded. Using both hands, Murray started to pull Jones from the pool. The boy did what he could to help him, but there were no footholds in the steep, slippery mud of the sides. Murray's arms began to burn with the strain of the sodden weight of the young man, and he could feel his shoulders being stretched beyond bearing. Slowly, inch by inch, Jones rose up from the water. Just when Murray thought he could bear no more and would have to let him go, the boy got one hand on the edge of the pit, then two, then pulled himself the rest of the way over and tumbled over the edge into the shallow safety behind the lip of the shell hole.

Murray clasped his shoulder with aching fingers and pointed back towards their own lines. He gestured to show the boy they must make their way back slithering from dip to dip. The sky was beginning to lighten now. Soon they would be easily seen by the Germans, and then the best they could hope for would be a day pinned down in No Man's Land until somebody came out to rescue them that night. That was the best. The likelihood would be a bomb, a machine-gun bullet or a sniper's careful shot, and then there'd be nothing for anyone to rescue.

He gestured for Boy to move ahead of him, and they began their painstaking way away from the crater, and towards the suddenly attractive shapes of their own barbed wire entanglements.

Boy slithered ahead like a water rat, moving from dip to dip, from one small hummock or clump of soil to the next. Murray followed behind. He felt deadly tired. Every thread of light in the sky seemed to make him colder, heavier, less able to move. Twice Boy had to turn and come for him, tugging him along through the slime.

At last they reached the barbed wire. Murray had no idea where the gap was, and no energy to find it.

He started composing a letter to Miranda in his head:

Sorry, Turnip Top. Don't think I'm getting out of this one. Last night, up and over the top, we were told, and we did, and then all sorts happened, Turnip, and here I am, so bloody tired, and I'd so much rather be at home with you by the fire.

Murray's thoughts rambled on, and he dropped down into the mud. Boy shook him by the shoulder, first gently, then urgently, and pointed further down the barbed wire to where there was a gap. It was broad day now, and the sentries on both sides were jumpy with tiredness and terror. Was this the time when the enemy was going to launch an attack?

Murray's head buzzed with exhaustion, but he nodded to the boy and began slowly, slowly to squirm along towards the gap in the barbed wire. Jones wriggled ahead of him, ducked, slithered and was through, sliding over the parapet into the trench.

Murray followed inch by inch, and must have been nine, ten feet away from the gap when he felt a heavy weight slam into his back. He was hammered down into the mud and thought wryly that the sergeant had been right, you don't hear the one that gets you.

In a way it was a relief. He didn't have to move any more, and he felt warm and sleepy. Then the pain suddenly attacked him, washing over him in waves, and he heard a voice, his own, moaning. He tried to move, but something seemed wrong with his legs, and every time he tried to raise an arm or even just move his hand, searing hot agony swept up his back and down his legs. He was nailed to the mud, within just over a body's length of the parapet and safety, and he might as well have been on the moon. He thought a little, but he couldn't see anything anymore. Well, Turnip, it really is goodbye then.

CHAPTER 3

The glade in the wood was never quite silent, but there was never really any noise which the boy could name. Just rustlings, twitters, sharp cries, and the sound of the last leaves falling around him where he lay, curled on the rough blanket which the man had brought for him.

The boy had no idea how long he had lain there, nor how often the man had come to visit him, bringing food and slightly musty water, to be drunk from an army canteen, battered and scuffed with age.

At first he didn't really mind. The man was odd, muttering more to himself than speaking to him, but the boy had bread and boiled eggs and wrinkled old radishes to eat, water to drink, and the world around him to watch. It was better than being squeezed into the tiny cottage that was his home, between his sisters, giggling behind their hands about things he didn't understand and didn't care about, and his mother, silent most of the time unless to bark out orders or to find fault. He had run away that day to fish, to find some peace away from the cottage at the place he remembered his father had once sat. Or, at least, he thought he remembered, because his father had gone months, years ago, swallowed up into the big blue mass of the army, and no-one seemed to know where he was now or whether he was coming back. Or, if they did know, no-one was telling him.

So the boy and the man struck up some sort of pact. The boy would not leave the clearing in the woods, the man would bring him food and drink and sometimes sit with him to watch the animals as they went about their ways.

***

The major had not slept well. Even a small snifter of his carefully hoarded Lagavulin had not done the trick. His head was too full of all that he had seen and heard the day before. What had to be done. What must not be done. What it meant for the men under his command. What it meant for the men in his care. What it would mean for the men soon to be in his care.

He had tried to shake off his sense of terrible anxiety by getting up early the next morning, sluicing himself in the icy water of the pump, then giving himself a careful shave and a thoroughly good talking to. It was no good going around in a funk, putting the wind up himself with worrying about what might or might not happen. There were plans to be made, orders to be given, jobs to be done, and those were his immediate and pressing responsibility. It's not as if he didn't know what to do - for God's sake, he'd been at this game long enough, and had seen enough one way or another along the way. Malakand on the North West Frontier had been no picnic, what with the way the tribesmen - and, God knows, the tribeswomen - treated their prisoners. Poor devils.

The major shrugged and settled down at his desk. It was a rum job, being a doctor in a fighting army, patching people up so that they could go out and get hurt again. He'd been doing it for thirty years, at home, in the Sudan, in India, but nothing had so shaken him as this damned show, with the chlorine gas, and the mustard gas, and the high explosives. The human body didn't stand a chance against these weapons - nor the human mind. Damn it, he slammed his hand down on the pile of papers in front of him. Stop being an old woman and get the bloody job done, man. God knows, the poor sods coming in would need all the help they could get in a few days' time.

***

Madeleine had prepared the basket, with its few scrawny sprouts and a handful of eggs. She was just tying her scarf under her chin, against the cold wind that was beginning to rise, when the kitchen doorway darkened and Olivier stepped over the sill.

'Afternoon, Olivier, good of you to come. I'm just off to fetch little Alex from mama's. Could you see to the orchard, do you think? It's well past due being tidied up.'

'Afternoon, Madeleine,' grunted the broad-shouldered old man. 'Leave it to me. You be off now.'

Madeleine smiled at him distractedly, and hurried off across the yard and through the gate.

Olivier watched her go. She was a good one, strong and sensible, dealing with it all as only a good woman could. She'd held everything together since Alexandre had been killed, keeping things going, keeping things growing, even now, when the stables were full of groaning men instead of warm horses. Olivier trudged over to the shed, and fetched the heavy old rake, then out through the far gate at the back of the yard and into the orchard. There were leaves to be gathered, trees to be tended. Sometime, some year, there would be animals to feed again. There would be birth and growth, instead of this war, these deaths.

***

Dusk was falling when Madeleine got back to the farm with little Alex. Her mother had kept her gossiping, and the young woman had been loath to leave the older woman alone, the house chill and winter shadows gathering. But Alex had to go to bed, the last chores of the night had to be done, and her mother, after all, was well used to getting by.

Alex scampered into the kitchen and over to the embers still glowing in the fireplace. He stretched his arms out towards the warmth, leaving a trail of boots and scarf and coat behind him, knowing his mother would pick them up and put them where they belonged. Even when his mother grumbled and told him he was more than

41

old enough to look after his things properly, he didn't really hear the words, confident as he was in the abiding, unbreakable love that lay beneath them.

***

Madeleine had been the first of the girls to be married. Her sisters, older, more solid, more daunting in their certainties, had their followers, to be sure, but there was no suitor, it seemed, quite sure they wanted a lifetime of that assured decisiveness, however comforting the warmth of their wide hips. Madeleine, though, smiled more, was more pliable, more enthusiastic, and so the young men of the village vied for her favours. She only had eyes for one, though. Tall, silent Alexandre, with his downcast eyes and his beautiful, capable fingers, as he offered magical carvings he had made from wood he had found around the edges of his father's farm. Birds, rabbits, foxes, slowly, over the months, the little shelf over her bed was filled with wild things, leaping, gazing, crouching, pouncing, playing. All the wonder which she felt at the world around her Alexandre had captured in the wood. And so he won her heart, silently. They were married within the year, and little Alexandre was born ten months later. Then came the war. Alexandre had been among the first from the village to go. He had been in the reserves, had no reasons to oppose to the sergeant when he came to fetch him, had simply to pack his little bag, kiss his wife and baby son, and set off walking, setting his stride to the sergeant's.

Madeleine never saw him again.

A letter came, which the curé read to her. 'Missing, believed killed.' What does that mean, she'd asked. Have they lost him? Will he come home? No, my child, the curé had tried to explain without actually saying the words. It means that they cannot find his body. The shells, you know, the explosives, they destroy everything.

Then the war came closer, she heard the shells, she saw from afar the torn soil, the stripped trees, the barren wastes, and she understood.

Every day she played with little Alex at bedtime, laying out on his coverlet all the animals his father had made and telling stories of the magical forest where the little boy's father was living now, surrounded by wild things who brought him food and water, leaves to cover him, boughs to shelter him when the rains came. It was a good place, a safe place, a magical place, and one day all three of them, Maman, Papa and little Alex, would all live there together when the men and the guns had gone.

Slowly Alex's eyes would close, and she would place the carvings carefully back on the shelf and lie down beside her son, holding her to him, feeling in his warmth the lost warmth of her tall, silent husband, feeling in his sweet, solid little limbs an echo of the once sweet flesh of her lost lover.

Then, when she was sure Alex was properly asleep, Madeleine would rise and face the world as it was now.

She would go out into the yard and make sure the last few hens were safely shut away, from the foxes and from the hungry soldiers who sometimes came scrounging around the farm. She would go into the field behind the house and call in their last cow, lovely, bewildered Nanette, who couldn't quite grasp that she really was alone, and kept looking every night, and every morning, for the friends she had grown up with. She would low quietly, but always came obediently to Madeleine's call. Perhaps her friends were already in the shed, waiting for her? But now, there was always just the empty stall, the manger was filled with hay for her alone, the trough had fresh water just for her. She'd shake her head and settle for the night in the dark shed, as Madeleine padlocked the door behind her. She didn't understand. She never would.

Madeleine drew off her clothes, shivered as she pulled on her rough flannel nightshirt, and slipped gratefully into the warm bed beside her sleeping son.

In the wood, another boy settled down in bed, bracken and dried leaves beneath him. He heard the snuffling and the rustling of the night-time animals, the comfortable sounds of birds settling to roost, and fell asleep.

CHAPTER 4

3rd November, morning

It was only when Murray had been awake for a little while that he realised he was no longer lying in the cold mud. He was, he accepted without understanding, lying on a bed in a barn, and he was, as far as he could tell, no longer in pain.

A pale, fair-haired man was leaning over him and checking a huge bandage wound about his waist. Murray tried to sit up and cried out in sudden agony. So the pain hadn't really gone away - it had been an ambush. Hmm.

The man held Murray's shoulder.

'Best if you don't move just now. You've had a hell of a close one, and your back's in just a bit of a mess. Best thing you can do is sleep now. The medic'll be along again in a while and'll give you something more for the pain.'

Murray closed his eyes. He had no idea what was happening, and found himself caring not at all. So long as he was still, and it was quiet, he was content.

***

Jack made his way along the rows of wounded, checking dressings, adjusting pillows, murmuring words of comfort. He was about half-way down the ward when the doorway by the courtyard darkened. He looked over to see the major standing there and beckoning to him. With a last quick glance to make sure the lad he was tending to was comfortable, Jack followed the major out into the crisp light of the winter morning.

'Sir?' he asked, raising hand to brow in an approximate salute. As a member of the Brigade, he didn't really need to salute, but he and all the other nursing volunteers were to all intents and purposes members of the major's unit and under his command. And anyway, he rather admired the stocky, no-nonsense, highly competent doctor.

'Jack, I need to have a quiet and confidential word about how things need to go here in the next few days.'

The major led Jack across the courtyard, until they were both leaning on the gate which led into the orchard and, from there, into the fields beyond.

Neither could help resting their eyes on the horizon, where the stark skeletons of shattered trees and broken buildings marked the tideline where the army had broken through and driven the Huns back that spring.

'Thing is, Jack,' began the major, his eyes fixed on the distant devastation, 'there's going to be another push.'

Jack turned to the major, struck by the quiet seriousness of his tone.

'It's going to be a different kind of show, though. No big barrages for days on end, no massive mines like at Messines. This is going to be a softly, softly catchee monkey kind of do, according to HQ. All very hush hush, and the Hun mustn't get a hint of what's going on.'

The major paused. Jack reached for his cigarettes and offered one to the major. After they'd both lit up and taken a deep drag of the harsh tobacco, the major went on.

'I'll be briefing the rest of the unit this afternoon. There's going to be a lot to do - all the patients need to be shunted out - back to their units or up to the Base Hospital. Bedding cleaned, supplies topped up, what can be cleaned needs to be scrubbed up, what can't be cleaned needs to be replaced. Everything needs to be made ready. We've just a few days, maybe a couple of weeks, and then who knows what we'll be faced with.'

The major paused again, and turned to look Jack in the eye.

'Jack, you're quick, intelligent, and I know I can trust you.'

Jack looked down awkwardly, afraid he might be blushing at the unexpected praise.

'I want you to do something for me,' the major continued, feigning not to notice the young man's embarrassment. 'I want you to slip into the village as soon as you can - today's market day - and I want you to quietly and discreetly, without making a fuss, buy up anything you see that you think we could use when the balloon goes up. Linens for bandages, woollen blankets, and anything edible that'll last and provide nourishment. Pick up what you can without drawing attention - you speak the lingo, spin some kind of yarn, and do your best. You may not find much, and HQ is supposed to be sending us supplies, but I'd rather make our own arrangements as well, as far as we are able.'

The major reached into his breast pocket and fished out his wallet.

'Here's some spending money. Keep a record and let me have any change when you get back. Look lively, lad, and off you go. I'll take over where you left off on the ward.'

Jack pocketed the money, sketched out another salute somewhere in the region of his cap, and turned to walk thoughtfully into the village.

***

It was market day, and Madeleine had errands to run. She had tied Alex to her with a rope going from his wrist to hers. Though heaven knows it wasn't as busy as it had been in the days before the war, but there were still crowds milling around in the square and in the surrounding streets, crowds swelled by soldiers on leave and all the mix of men and women trying to sell them things, from tobacco to sex.

Madeleine had eggs to sell, and a few branches of sprouts. She had no idea what she would bring next week. Perhaps she could have a word with Marie-Laure and see whether they could sell a few of her mother-in-law's old knick-knacks and share the proceeds between them. Though who would want porcelain carthorses or china violets in a tiny vase? But there had to be some solution, since anything else was unthinkable.

The market square was full of stalls, and, for a moment, it was possible to imagine that the war had never happened and that the life she had always known was proceeding in its steady, regular way.

There was Mme Bauvais with her garlic and onions, still laid out in elegant patterns on the red and white checks of her tablecloth. There was M. Lenclos with his cheeses, rows upon rows, each with a small knife across it, so that customers could sample before buying. There was Geraldine Pokily, one of Madeleine's oldest friends, selling her linen pillowcases, sheets and cloths. Beautifully sewn as always, and laid in solid slabs of white across the stall.

It was only when you went close that you could see how little there was actually for sale, and how each of the stallholders had spread out their wares to cover their stalls as much as possible and to disguise the thinness of their offerings.

And then, if you looked around, you noticed that all the stallholders were women or old men, with a few children helping out here and there. All the men, and there were scores of them, wandering in knots, fondling the market wares with wondering fingers, all the men were in uniform, and none of them belonged.

Madeleine blinked as she always did, even after all this time, on seeing the soldiers. Where was her Alexandre? Was he wandering some strange market town, looking at unfamiliar wares? She hoped desperately that it was so. She knew, to the core of her being, that it was not.

***

The man sat at the dusty table. His hands clasped a mug of coffee, his eyes rested on the woods beyond the window, his lips moved as if in prayer. 'Paul, François, Michel, Jean-Marie, Philippe, Claude, Gabriel, Jean-Baptiste, Alexandre, Gustave.' These ones he'd seen, these he knew he must help.

***

Jack had moved about the market as discreetly as he could, buying linen sheets here, cheeses there, onions at a third stall, until he had spent almost all of the major's money, and had a solid collection of useful items. He had noticed early on the woman from the farm moving through the crowds, her little boy at her side, chatting here and there as she passed friends out shopping and stallholders she knew.

When Jack had bought all that he could buy, he hired an old man with a handcart to deliver everything back to the major at the CCS, saying he would follow on behind.

Pretending to himself that it was nothing more than idle curiosity, Jack looked around to see if he could spot the dark-haired woman and her little boy. Ah, there she was, her errands run, carrying a basket with a few small items in it, and tugging along the little boy, who seemed reluctant to leave the crowded market to go back to the quiet of the farm.

Jack shouldered through the thinning crowd and made his way over to the pair where they stood, she struggling to set off home, he digging his heels into the road in mutinous recalcitrance.

Using his best Parisian accent and big city manners, Jack introduced himself.

'Good morning, madame,' he said, doffing his cap and offering her a slight bow. 'My name is Jack. I am one of the nurses at the CCS. It seems as though you have a mutineer on your hands.'

Man and woman together looked down at little Alex, where he now sat in the dusty roadway, something like triumph gleaming in his dark eyes at having brought his mother to a full stop.

Jack crouched down until he was looking little Alex in the eye.

'What would you say to having a ride back to the farm on my shoulders? You can be a cavalryman and I'll be your charger. Would that be alright with you, madame?' Jack asked, looking up at Madeleine.

Alex had already jumped up and was scrabbling his way onto Jack's shoulders. Madeleine, smiling, untied the rope from the little boy's wrist and held out a hand to help Jack get to his feet.

He seemed very frail, this gaunt, fair-haired Englishman, with his perfect French and his polished manners. There were dark shadows under his pale eyes, and he was struggling not to cough, with Alex's sturdy little heels drumming into his chest. But then he grinned, and a wonderful sharp light seemed to wash over his features, giving her a glimpse of the man he must once have been, and perhaps one day might be again.

Together the man, the woman and the little boy made their way back to the farm.

CHAPTER 5

3rd November, afternoon

Time passed. The boy began to wander from the glade. He understood, though nothing had been said, that this was a breach of trust, that the man expected him to stay, but the boy grew restive, all the hours on his own - he even, in an unformed, shapeless way, missed his sisters and his silent, admonishing mother. He was careful, though, at first, planning his forays so that he left the clearing only after the last sounds of the man's retreating footsteps had died away following one of his visits, and never going so far that he couldn't scurry back when he heard him trudging heavy-footed, returning through the fallen leaves. But there came, of course, the moment when the boy lost track of time.

The man came to the glade and found the child gone. He thought at first that the boy was asleep under the pile of blankets and old coats that he had brought for him and laid out in the rough lean-to shaped from logs and branches and stolen planks of wood. He went into the hut and gently shook the bundle, but there was no small shape dozing underneath.

The man left the hut and began to peer around the edges of the glade, muttering, sniffing like a hound searching for a scent. He couldn't see the boy. His muttering grew more urgent, his steps swifter, and then he saw him. The child was crouched on a rock, looking down, watching, the man saw as he drew closer, a nest of ants, hurrying, carrying tiny twigs, bits of leaves, moving in a wavering line, up the rock and down, building their nest. The man walked quietly up behind the boy and squatted beside him. Together they watched the ants. A companionable silence seemed to fall, but there was tension between them. The boy was waiting for the reprimand, the heavy cuff across the cheeks which always met any breaking of the rules at home.

The man was puzzling how best to proceed, how to carry out his careful plan. Eventually, saying nothing, he picked the boy up and carried him back to the clearing. The boy remained silent, not afraid, exactly, but unsure. He sat while the man rooted around in the hut and came out with a length of rope. Silently, he tied one end to a tree at the edge of the clearing, then fastened the other tightly, but not harshly, round the boy's waist.

The boy stood, tethered, looking at the man as he checked the knots on the rope. For the first time, the man spoke to him directly. 'You must not leave. Stay, always stay.' The man laid a hand on the boy's slight shoulder and shook him lightly. 'Stay, yes?' The boy nodded. What choice did he have?

***

Jack's shoulders ached, and he had bruises on his chest. He had lifted his shirt and checked in the mirror. The sight made him smile. He hadn't felt so alive since he honestly couldn't remember when. And wasn't that the paradox? His smile became a tinge ironic. Ah well, it had been nice while it lasted. Giving himself a slight shake he made his way across the courtyard to the barn full of dead and dying, maimed and mutilated men.

There were already fewer men lying there than there had been when he set off to the market that morning. The major's broom had started to sweep efficiently clean. The lieutenant with the nasty gash in his back was still there though. He was moaning between clenched teeth, his eyes tight shut, and his dark hair black with sweat.

'Hey, old man,' Jack bent over the wounded man, laying a cool and gentle hand on his forehead. The soldier was burning up. 'Let me just check your dressings.'

Jack called over another of the ward orderlies, and, with enormous care, they turned the lieutenant on his side, and Jack pulled back the dressing on his wound. A piece of shrapnel had sliced across his back from right shoulder to left hip, missing severing the spinal cord by fractions of a whisker.

'Go and fetch the major, will you? I'm not sure what's the best thing to do here.'

The major strode quickly into the half-empty ward and stood beside the feverish lieutenant's bedside. He leant over and carefully examined the wound.

'There seems to be some inflammation here,' he said. 'See this area of redness just above the lumbar region? The wound was debrided very efficiently when he first came in, but it looks as though a tiny bit of something nasty has been missed.'

The major walked round the foot of the bed, and crouched so that the shivering patient could see and hear him properly.

'It's going to be fine, lad. You've got a bit of an infection in the wound, so I'm going to knock you out, clean it up and have a bit of a rummage around to make sure there's nothing else lurking. You'll be out for about thirty minutes, and you'll hurt like buggery for the rest of the day, but after that you'll be as right as rain.'

He straightened up and ordered the operating theatre to be readied. The wounded man was stretchered into the little walled off area that had once been the tack room, and the anaesthetics officer administered the nitrous oxide.

The operation was over in twenty minutes, and the patient, freshly dressed and between clean sheets, lay on his side, still unconscious and very pale.

Jack posted an orderly at the man's bedside. 'Call me when he begins to stir.'

***

In the farmhouse kitchen, Olivier sat with little Alex in front of the fire, while Madeleine stood at the table preparing the vegetables for supper.

Olivier shook his shoulders and rested his hand on Alex's head.

'Well, my boy, we'd better go and get those trees seen to before it gets too dark. They really should have been done weeks ago. We mustn't let any more time slip by.'

He tousled the boy's hair, and turned to Madeleine.

'We'll be in the orchard if you need us.'

Madeleine nodded and watched as the tall man led her slender son across the courtyard.

'Now, lad,' she heard him say. 'We're going to need sacking, a sharp knife, a ball of twine and a bucketful of axle grease. Oh, and old gloves for thee and me, or your mother'll be after us both with a rolling pin.'

Madeleine smiled to herself, and bent back to her vegetables.

The old man and the small boy gathered together their supplies and made their way through the gate into the orchard. Leaves lay piled where Olivier had raked them the day before, ready to light a bonfire when the time was right.

'What are we going to do with all this stuff?' Alex asked the old man.

'With this stuff, as you call it, we're going to protect mama's fruit trees from all sorts of naughty grubs.'

'But there aren't any grubs around at the moment, are there?' asked Alex, eager to understand. 'Isn't it too cold for grubs now?'

'Yes indeed it is, but it's not too cold for their mamas. Some moths, like the winter moths, wait for November and December to lay their eggs, so that there'll be lots of lovely soft fresh leaf buds for their babies to feed on.'

Olivier laid the sacking on the ground, and swiftly cut it into strips. As he worked, he went on explaining to Alex. 'The mummy moths don't have any wings, and, until they're ready to lay their eggs, they snooze quietly underground at the foot of the tree, until it's chilly

54

enough to wake them up and to set them off climbing up the tree to lay their eggs among the branches where the leaves and fruit will grow. But if we do this,' and he picked up one of the strips of sacking and tied it around the trunk of an apple tree, about a foot off the ground, fastening it securely with a length of twine, 'and then we do this,' and he lathered the cloth liberally with axle grease, 'then the mummy moth can't climb over the slippery grease to lay her eggs, and the eggs can't turn into maggots that feast away on the budding leaves. The tree is kept safe, and in the spring we can take the grease bands off again.'

Alex followed the man from tree to tree, watching him at work. He seemed unusually thoughtful.

'So, Monsieur Olivier,' said the little boy at length, 'if we had had a big enough grease band, we could have put it down so that the Boches wouldn't have been able to get over it, and my daddy wouldn't have had to go off to fight them.'

Olivier turned and looked at the little boy, his expression caught halfway between sorrow and a smile.

'Why, yes, little lad. When you grow up you ought to be a general.'

Alex shook his head vehemently. 'No! I'll never, ever be a soldier. Soldiers are smelly and dirty. They're noisy, thieving, horrible men. And they get hurt.'

'But your daddy was a soldier, wasn't he, Alex? And he wasn't a dirty, smelly thief, was he?'

'No,' replied the boy. 'But he did get hurt, didn't he?'

The tall old man found he had no answer to that.

CHAPTER 6

7th November, overnight and early morning

The night was dark, with the last quarter of the waning moon struggling to show its light between the scudding clouds. And, in the darkness, men moved with silent urgency as troops and guns made their way as quietly and secretly as they could to their new positions.

***

In the CCS, nothing could be heard of the muttered orders and muffled footsteps, or the rumble of heavy wheels along the road at the foot of the driveway leading to the farm. Here, in the barn, men moaned and mumbled, the medical staff tiptoed round with torches, dispensing medication or a soothing word. It was that liminal time when the world felt poised between dark and light, the night dragging to its slow end, the day as yet unformed.

Murray lay with his eyes closed, listening to the soft sounds all around him. For the last three days, since he came round from the operation, he had been playing a game with himself. If he could guess correctly what a man looked like just from his voice, he awarded himself 5 points. If he could guess where he was wounded, another 5 points. If he guessed correctly whether or not they would survive the night, that was 20 points. Over the three days and nights he'd been playing, he reckoned he had accumulated 120 points. He had made some mistakes, but he hadn't worked out a proper system of penalties, and somehow he didn't want to. He had guessed wrongly that the white-faced Welshman with red hair was going to last the night, and had, indeed, hoped he would, because he'd been enjoying chatting to him in a fragmented, desultory way. Waking the previous morning to find the man's bed empty and the orderlies carrying his still form, covered in a sheet, out to the makeshift mortuary in the creamery, was penalty enough, Murray reckoned.

Murray sighed, and wondered what had happened to Boy. He had no memory at all of moving from where he had been lying just short of the barbed wire entanglements, deciding that enough was enough, and waking where he was now - wherever that was - lying in the shelter of an old barn, surrounded by cries and moans, and being handled by almost silent men with surprisingly gentle hands.

He shifted himself, as far as he could, so that he lay on his side, his arms tucked underneath the covers. He could just see the light changing in the doorway into the yard beyond. Sunrise. It seemed a world away.

***

Jack's sleep had been disturbed, partly because of the unfamiliar sounds coming from the road, and partly because his head was spinning with all that had been done and all that still remained to do. It didn't help that they had, of course, no idea when the attack would be launched, or where, or what the objectives were. All that they did know was that the Powers That Be were trying something new, and that they were quite excited about it.

He got up and sluiced his head under the icy water of the pump in the yard in an attempt to clear out the cobwebs. Towelling himself down in the crisp morning air, he saw little Alex loitering by the farmhouse door.

'Good morning,' he said to the boy, rather hoping that his dark-eyed mother might not be far away. 'What are you up to this fine autumn day?'

Alex grinned up at him.

'I'm going with Olivier to put netting over the cabbages and the sprouts, to save them from soldiers like you!'

'Well, Alex,' said Olivier, coming out from the farmhouse and into the courtyard. 'That's only partly true. The netting is mainly to stop the pigeons eating the few vegetables we have left - but if it stops some of the thieving soldiers as well, so much the better! Not that this fine young man is a soldier, Alex. He is a member of the St John Ambulance Brigade - and I am sure he has never stolen a brussel sprout in his life!'

Olivier grinned at Jack. Jack replied, 'I can say, hand on heart,' matching the action to the word, 'I have never stolen a brussel sprout. The occasional apple might have slipped off the tree into my pocket when I was a boy, but a sprout, never!'

Olivier nodded and put his hand on the little boy's shoulder. 'Come on, my lad, we need to go and sit like a couple of old fishermen, and untangle our nets and mend any holes we find.'

The little boy scampered through the gate and over to the shed where the netting was kept. Olivier waved a hand in farewell to Jack and strode after him.

Jack stood a moment in the empty courtyard, before bracing his shoulders and turning to go into the barn, and the rows of wounded men.

***

Alex had gone into the farmhouse to have his lunch. Olivier had chosen to have his - a hunk of bread and some good strong cheese - leaning on the orchard gate, looking over to the devastated horizon where once a thriving little town had stood. Beyond, out of sight, lay the front line. And beyond that, dug in deep, lay the Germans.

He sighed and reached into his pocket for his pipe. He was just about to get out his tobacco pouch when the little English doctor came up and leant on the gate beside him, offering him a fill of his own pipe tobacco, which smelt amazing.

'Greek,' explained the major. 'My tobacconist keeps a special supply for me. Yenidji. Really smooth with a bit of a sting in the tail. Would you care to try some?'

'Thank you, major, that is very generous,' replied Olivier, reaching out and taking a modest fill. He stuffed his pipe, and then stood for a while appreciating the aroma of the exotic tobacco before setting a match to it.

'If you don't mind my saying so,' began the major hesitantly, 'you speak excellent English.'

'Thank you again,' Olivier inclined his head graciously. 'I wasn't always, what do you say, a country bumpkin.'

He smiled, and the stocky little doctor, his curiosity awakened, smiled back.

'No? And what were you then, before you became a country bumpkin?' giving the words an ironic emphasis.

'I was a policeman, right down in the south, in Lyons.'

'And, if you'll forgive my assumption, a fairly senior one too, I'll be bound,' said the major, looking up at his companion with a considering, intelligent eye.

'Indeed, for what it's worth,' conceded Olivier, 'I was a commandant in the Sûreté - I think that is something equivalent to a superintendent in your police forces.'

'And, forgive me again, my curiosity's got the better of me,' said the major with a show of diffidence, ' how does an ex-superintendent from the Lyons Sûreté come to be acting as a handyman on a farm in the middle of a war zone in northern France?'

'It is not an exciting story, but, if you really are interested, I'll be happy to tell you.' Olivier found himself drawn to the charming, insistent doctor, and was rather enjoying having a conversation about something more than turnips and coddling moths.

'As you may know, no member of the police forces in France, whether the police, the gendarmerie or the Sûreté, may be posted to their home area. The theory is that it avoids prejudice and being open to pressure from friends and family, and instead encourages a disinterested objectivity. And that may be the case. Who knows? The fact is that I was born here, in this village, and so, when I passed my exams and was accepted into the Sûreté, they sent me pretty much as far away as they could.

'I enjoyed my time in Lyons - good weather, good food, and a big enough city to provide a constant, varied range of villains. In fact, while I was there, I had some very interesting and useful conversations with a professional colleague of yours.'

The major cocked his head questioningly.

'A man called Edmond Locard. Heard of him?'

The major shook his head.

'A damn clever fellow,' went on Olivier. 'A doctor and a qualified lawyer. Red hot on using science to solve crimes. Developed an interesting theory about how you always leave evidence of your presence in a place - and take evidence with you too. The Exchange Principle, he called it. He had a kind of catch-phrase, "Every contact leaves a trace".

'Had a splendid system for identifying fingerprints using the impressions left by the pores, too. His system was sufficiently rigorous that it was accepted by the courts - just twelve specific points identical between two fingerprints, and it simply had to be the same person. And you know how the layman likes a little bit of science sprinkled over his salad. "I wasn't there!" pleads René. "Ah, but your hands were - bang him up!" replies the magistrate. Lovely!'

'Fingerprints, eh?' remarked the major, looking down at his hands inquisitively. 'Fascinating, absolutely fascinating. But I still don't quite understand why you're up here doing odd jobs for Madame, rather than being down south, drinking fine wine and banging up the bad boys.'

'Well, it was a combination of two, or even three things,' replied Olivier. 'First of all, my mother, who'd been widowed for many years, was getting increasingly frail and a little bit, how shall I put it, confused. I'm an only child, and although I've got cousins galore round about, it didn't feel right not being there to take care of her myself. Then I wasn't getting any younger myself, and, truth to tell, I was beginning to feel just a little bit jaded with the endless stream of unimaginative, idiotic felons I had to deal with. If only some of them could have been even just a little bit original!' Olivier threw up his hands in exaggerated despair. 'And finally, of course, there was the war. Locard was co-opted by the Secret Service to help pin down how and where casualties had died from the stains and damage on unidentified soldiers' remains. They asked if I'd like to go too, but I couldn't face it. Can you imagine, lost, broken bodies, day after day?'

He looked at the major, and saw the doctor's sombre expression.

'Of course you can. That's all you deal in day in, day out. Sorry for being so crass, old man.'

'It's different, though,' said the major, acknowledging Olivier's embarrassed apology. 'At least I have the chance of saving some of them.'

'Well, be that as it may, the long and the short of it is that I resigned the service, picked up my pension, and came back to look after my poor old ma. And in my spare time, I put my hand to whatever else needs doing roundabout. Lots of fresh air and a blessed absence of villains - apart, of course, from that lot over there,' nodding his head towards the horizon and the massed German army.

'Talking of which,' said the major, 'I better get back to the boys, and put them back together so that they can go out and get shot to bits again, poor silly, benighted buggers. Thanks, old man.' The major held out his hand to the ex-policeman. 'Very good to know you. Good man and all that, eh?' and embarrassed at his own effusiveness, the major fled across the courtyard and onto the ward in the barn.

At first, the boy would go as far into the edge of the forest as the rope would allow, and sit still, watching, as before, the insects and small animals making their busy way across the forest floor.

He had always been fascinated by the fields and woods around his home, slipping away from the chores around the house as often as he could, simply to sit and watch. Sometimes, when his father had been home, they'd gone together.

Gradually, though, he sank into indifference, and would stay where the man last left him after feeding him and setting a fresh water container at his side. He left torn paper, too, for the boy to wipe himself with. Now his world had just three parts to it - where he relieved himself, carefully covering each dropping with leaves and soil; where he sometimes sat to watch the ants and voles; and the pile of coats and blankets where he lay, dozing, sleeping, or just not moving. The man had bent more branches over the nest of blankets, and covered them with leaves and twigs, so that even when it rained the boy could be dry and sheltered.

Soon his world contracted to two spots - his nest and where he relieved himself.

The man became concerned at the boy's torpor, and started to prod him to his feet when he came on his visits, dragging him around in a circle by the rope bound round his waist to make him exercise. The boy didn't resist, but he didn't cooperate either. He walked, leaden stepped and leaden eyed, or stumbled if the man pulled harder to make him go faster. Sometimes the man grew irritated, and cuffed the boy, but he always cried afterwards, cradling the child's head against his shoulder and murmuring inarticulate sounds of comfort.

The man brewed a tonic to give the boy, from mushrooms and herbs and dried pig's blood.

The boy drank and was sick. The man gave him water, and then another mug of the tonic again. The boy drank and seemed to revive slightly, looking around him as though seeing the clearing for the first time. After a while he looked at the man.

'I'd like to go home now,' he said.

'No, no,' said the man. The words felt strange in his mouth. He didn't speak often to anyone, and he had hardly spoken to the boy at all.

The boy's eyes filled with tears. He made no noise, but two wet streaks ran down his cheeks, clear channels in the grime and muck that caked his face. Then the boy's mouth opened, and a huge yell erupted into the small clearing, followed by another and another. The boy screamed and thrashed about, kicking out at the man who knelt beside him.

'Home,' he screamed. 'I want to go home. I want Mama. I want to go home. I want to go home. I want to go home.'

The man sought to still him and comfort him as he would a frightened horse or a nervous dog. His huge hand held the boy's small shoulders, while he made inarticulate soothing sounds deep in his throat.

The boy thrashed and screamed, beyond comfort, beyond reason, beyond help.

The sound was more than the man could bear.

He laid his hand across the boy's mouth to silence the noise.

The boy bit at the man's hand.

The man tightened his grip across the child's face and around his neck.

And then the boy grew still.

The man looked down at the small figure, and laid it gently down on the blankets. The boy's head lay at a strange angle, but at least he was quiet now.

CHAPTER 7

8th November, overnight and early morning onwards

The man stayed sitting beside the small figure as the shadows fell and dusk turned into night. He sat beside the boy all the night through, hardly moving, at first numb, then full of rage and confusion, and then, finally, with a single clear purpose.

He knew now what he had to do. He had made a mistake before, keeping the child captive. That was wrong, and had made the boy frightened and unhappy.

As the dawn rose, the man stood awkwardly and bent to pick up the stiff, chill body of the child. Taking him in his arms a little way into the woods, he laid him down on the leaves.

The man went back to the clearing and fetched a hoe he'd stored there. He stepped quietly back beside the boy and, kneeling, scraped out a hole deep enough and long enough to hold the little figure. He laid the child in the cool rich earth. He didn't want him to be cold, though, when the snows came. Rising again, the man went back into the glade and fetched one of the blankets, covering the child gently. Then he tumbled the earth back into the hole and filled it. He found stones from round about, and covered the small mound to keep away the foxes. He scattered leaves and a few twigs over it until it was almost invisible, just another part of the mottled forest floor.

The man rose and dusted the soil and leaf mould from his hands.

***

While the man kept vigil by the child's body, the dark night covered the busy, surreptitious movements of multitudes of other men.

The attack, when it came, depended on surprise, and that meant that every soldier, every gun, every shell had to be moved up towards their final positions night by night, as silently as possible. Torches half covered, orders relayed in an undertone, the huge and heavy guns hauled inch by inch along the roads, until the lightening sky brought warning of daylight. In controlled haste, guns, men, ammunition, were all moved off the roads and into such shelter as they could find - buildings or woods or ruins - hunkered down or covered with netting against the chance of German spotter planes. Then stillness and silence until the next night came.

***

Murray was baffled. Baffled and angry. The nurse who tended him most of the time, a St John's volunteer called Jack, should surely have been in uniform? He seemed, as far as he could tell from where he lay in the gloom of the ward, to be perfectly fit, about the same age as Murray himself, and better officer material than many of the poor sods who ended up in the trenches, with their shiny Sam Browns and their well-oiled Webleys. So what the hell was he doing here, swanning about behind the lines, playing at Florence Nightingale?

The next time the fair-haired nurse came to tend to him, Murray turned his face away and met the man's questions about how he had slept and how much pain he was in with a stony silence. The nurse shrugged, jotted something down on his medical notes, and moved on to the next patient.

Murray hugged his anger to him. It fuelled his energy better than pain or fear. Once he was up and about he'd have it out with the shirker. Now, though, what he wanted above all was to get his carcass out of this damned bed.

He caught the eye of an orderly who was cleaning the ward.

'Any chance of a hand out of this bed and into a chair, old man?'

The orderly, still mopping the floor, looked over at Murray.

'You'll need to ask the major about that. He'll be round in a minute.'

And so it was that, later on that morning, Murray found himself being carefully helped into a wheelchair by the fair-haired nurse who had made him so angry earlier. He still was angry, but felt it prudent to be at least courteous to the man who was, at this point, quite literally supporting him.

Once safely propped into the wheelchair, with pillows and blankets tucked all around so that his back was kept as straight as possible, Murray asked whether he might sit in the courtyard for a while. It was nearly a week since he'd been wounded, and he found himself longing for daylight and fresh air.

The nurse wheeled him out into the courtyard, and found him a corner out of the wind where he could sit for a while.

'Just a moment,' said the nurse and hurried away.

He was back in a short while with a thick quilt. He tucked it all around Murray, making sure the back of his neck and his hands were covered.

'I just remember how bloody cold it got lying outside for hours on end when I was at the sanatorium.'

'Sanatorium?' Murray couldn't help but ask.

'Oh, yes.' The fair-haired man squatted beside Murray, back against the wall, and fumbled in a pocket for his packet of cigarettes. He offered one to Murray, and they both lit up.

'My name's Jack, by the way,' he said, reaching over to shake Murray by the hand. Murray kept his hands under the quilt. Jack paused a moment, shrugged and then went on, 'Strictly speaking I shouldn't be here at all, and I certainly shouldn't be smoking these ruddy gaspers. My doc'd have a fit if he saw me. TB, don't you know? Spent months sitting around in the icy cold being plied with strange herbal concoctions, so I do know just how bloody freezing it can be.'

Murray sat very silently for a bit, and then he turned as far as he could towards Jack.

'Jack,' he said in a serious voice, 'I owe you an apology.'

'I have no idea what you mean, old man.'

'Yes, I was hateful towards you first thing this morning, and I was pretty hateful towards you just now. I thought you were one of those ruddy conchies, and here you are a sick man doing your bit. Please accept my sincerest apologies, old fellow.'

Murray held his hand out to Jack, who shook it with a grin.

'Of course, I could be a sick man doing his bit and a ruddy conchie too,' he said teasingly. 'Don't think I am, though. Don't get me wrong - I can't stand war. Stupid, messy business. But I can't stand bullies either.'

With that, Jack stood up and stubbed his cigarette out underfoot, carefully picking up the dog-end and putting it in his pocket. There'd come a time when he'd be glad of those last few strands of tobacco.

'Ah well, duty calls,' he said. 'I'll be back in half an hour or so to put you back to bed. If you need anything in the meantime, just give me a shout.'

And with that Jack went back through the dark barn doorway.

Murray sat for a while simply relishing the quiet and the cold fresh air. He thought he could even hear the chirrup of a sparrow, but that might have been wishful thinking.

He must have dozed off, because the next thing he was aware of was a cold draft blowing down the back of his neck. Army-issue pyjamas were certainly not ideal outdoor wear. Looking down, he realised the quilt had slipped off, and was now lying in an ungainly heap beside his wheelchair. He was trying vainly to reach his hand down far enough to grab hold of it and pull it up again when he heard footsteps hurrying towards him. A dark-haired young woman - his age? Perhaps older? - was quickly crossing the courtyard. In a swift, efficient movement she retrieved the quilt, shook it out, and tucked it once again around his shoulders. She smiled at him diffidently and asked him a question.

'I am afraid I don't speak French,' Murray replied apologetically. 'Non parler français.'

The woman smiled, and said something more, and then, hesitantly, 'No speak English.'

'Ah, well,' said Murray, shrugging his shoulders. 'Thank you anyway. Merci, madame,' he added, nodding his head courteously.

The woman spoke again, patted him lightly on the shoulder as a gesture of farewell, and went quickly back into the farmhouse.

***

The morning drew on, and there seemed to be a kind of thickening in the air, as the troops who had marched up overnight gradually awoke from sleep, and began to look around them. They were billeted and bivouacked everywhere in and around the little village. Word was they'd be here a day or two before moving forward. But who knew? They might be off that evening or next Christmas. In the meantime they had a few hours' leisure to check their equipment, to stretch their legs, or simply to brew up a mug of tea.

Jack was gradually working his way down the list of tasks the major had given him. He'd sorted out bedding and bandages. Next on the list, medication. How much was there, and of what? All the drugs were kept locked up in a sluice room set up just outside the operating theatre.

Jack strode into the sluice room, his head full of everything that needed to be done before night fell, and stopped dead in surprise.

Kneeling in front of the drugs cabinet was a skinny, scruffy soldier, who looked as if he was trying to unlock the cabinet door.

'What the devil are you up to?' demanded Jack, shock giving an edge to his voice.

The soldier leapt up and spun round to face him.

69

'Oh sir, sorry sir, no harm meant, sir. Just looking for a bit of something to stop my feet hurting, sir. Terrible blisters I've got, sir, after last night's march.'

'What's your name, private?' asked Jack, surprising himself at how soldier-like he sounded.

'Slater, sir. Private Sidney. Post Office Rifles.' The man stood to attention and snapped out a reasonably respectable salute.

'Well, Private Sidney Slater, you better bugger off out of here double quick, and if I see you around here again, I'll be reporting you to your C.O. - oh, and by the way, if you've got blisters on your feet, just piss on them like everyone else does, there's a good fellow.'

The soldier saluted again and left. Jack was certain he'd been up to no good, but he'd been caught in time, and no harm done. Now, where had he put that list?

***

The man had not slept. He had gone back to the clearing once since burying the boy, and sat for a long while beside the tumble of stones and leaves which covered the small grave. He understood now that the boy had shown him something important. It needed to be done, of course, he'd always known that, but it needed to be done much more thoroughly and much more swiftly than he had realised. He had been unkind keeping the boy captive like that. That wouldn't happen again. He knew who he needed to protect, and now he knew how best to protect them.

He sat in his kitchen, checking that he had everything he needed and that it was all in perfect working order. His gun was cleaned and loaded. His knives sharpened and sheathed. He would be travelling a fair way backwards and forwards over the next few nights - water, cheese, some sausage, and a sack.

Fine. He was ready. It was time to go. He might even manage to make a start tonight.

CHAPTER 8

November 9th, morning onwards

Jack was delighted to find that his trip into the village fell at the same time as Madeleine had decided to walk over there to visit a friend.

Jack, as he told Madeleine, was on his way to beg, borrow or barter any drugs and herbs he could from the village pharmacist. Although the CCS had a lot of medicines which were supposed to be coming with the supplies in the next few days, the major was strongly of the opinion that you couldn't have too much of a good thing, and that almost anything at all was better than nothing.

Madeleine nodded her understanding, and said that she was going to see a friend of hers, Anne-Marie Mardel, who had a child almost the same age as Alex. She was desperately worried, because her little boy had been missing for nearly a week now, no-one had seen him and the police were saying they could do nothing.

'Why on earth not?' asked Jack indignantly.

Madeleine shrugged. 'They blame it on the war, of course. They can't mount a proper search, because the soldiers won't let them, they say. And the soldiers say they can't do anything, that it's a civilian matter. So Anne-Marie is left looking after the other children, and hunting for little Paul here and there whenever she can. He's just five years old!'

Madeleine dropped her voice so that Alex, running on a little ahead, would not be able to hear. 'Whatever has happened to Paul, after all this time, it can be nothing good.'

Jack felt almost irresistibly drawn to reach out to this quiet, thoughtful woman. He wanted to place his arms round her and to comfort her. Instead, he told her, in a subdued voice, 'Anything I can do to help, madame, please let me know.'

There fell a silence between them, full of an awareness of things unspoken, almost revealed, then they both gladly turned the conversation to other, easier topics. Soon they reached the village and parted ways, Madeleine and Alex to visit her desperate friend, Jack to see what kind of herbs, potions and lotions he could rustle up from the pharmacist.

***

The major was doing his best to follow orders. He could be seen in every quarter of the CCS, bustling about, muttering to himself.

'Sheets, yes we probably have enough sheets. Blankets? No, nowhere near enough, of course. Morphine? Possibly a week's supply, depending. And that's the whole question, isn't it? Depending on what? Depending on when? Prepare, they say, prepare. But prepare for bloody what? And bloody when?'

His intense monologue washed him up at Murray's bedside. This man, with his back torn open, was one of the few patients still remaining at the CCS.

Murray was sitting quietly on the side of his bed, trying to get some kind of movement into his stiff and incredibly sore back. He could barely move an inch, and he didn't trust his legs to hold him up. Or, to be more honest, he was terrified of the pain if he should try to stand, and then fell and jarred his back. Everything was just about manageable at the moment, but he had no idea how to, quite literally, take the next step.

'So, young fella,' said the major, looking down at the man as he sat on the edge of the bed, his hands gripping the coverlet, and his mouth clenched shut. 'You look as if you've something foolish in mind. Speaking as your doctor, I'd have to say that foolishness is contra-indicated. What exactly is it you're thinking of doing?'

Murray looked up at the major with something almost like a smile. 'I'm thinking of taking up my bed and walking, but both the taking up my bed and the walking bit seem a touch beyond me at the moment.'

'Well, lieutenant, we don't really do miracles here. The impossible, sometimes. The amazing, regularly. But miracles are not my specialisation, I'm afraid.' The major smiled at the pale young man, and carefully sat on the bed beside him. 'I do have a serious question to ask you, though.'

Murray turned towards the major, his eyes fixed on the doctor's earnest features.

'Thing is, my lad,' the major went on. 'You're sort of betwixt and between. You'll have noticed that all of the seriously wounded men have already been moved off to Base Hospital.'

Murray nodded.

'And most of the other lads have been patched up and sent back to their units. There's only fewer than a dozen of you left here, and I've got to make a decision what to do about you in the next couple of days. So, my question to you is, Base Hospital for as long as it takes, and perhaps even a chance of Blighty, or stay here a few more days or so and then back to your unit?'

Murray found himself answering before he'd even thought through the implications of the major's question. 'Not Base Hospital, thank you, sir. And certainly not Blighty - not at all sure how that'd be...' Murray's voice trailed off, as he thought of Miranda, and his mother, and the big house full of empty rooms and shadows. He pulled himself together. 'So, sir, if it's possible, I'd like to stay here for a few days, until I'm fit enough to go and rejoin my unit ready for the next Show. I don't imagine it'll be long in coming.'

The major smiled sadly, 'No, not long at all, I imagine. Well, that's decided then. We'll keep you here a couple of weeks, and then re-assess. Good man, good man.' The major stood and gave Murray a gentle pat on the shoulder before proceeding on his rounds, checking up on the ragtag of patients remaining.

***

The village was busier than usual for a weekday, with knots of soldiers here and there, wandering aimlessly, or standing gossiping quietly together. A lot of them looked bemused, as though they weren't quite sure how they had washed up in this strange island of normality and domesticity. There were houses here, with people, and shops, and, everywhere they looked, things seemed so ordinary. It was oddly unsettling.

Jack threaded his way between the slow-moving groups of men, and went into the pharmacist's. As he shut the door behind him, a bell clanged, and an elderly man came out from a back room and stood inquiringly behind the counter. For a moment, Jack just paused silently, drinking in the quiet and the wonderful fusty smells of herbs and lotions that filled the little shop. The pharmacist waited patiently. He was in no hurry. This fair-haired foreigner with the slightly feverish look would soon say what he needed. In the meantime, the stillness of the shop was by no means the least of the healing elements the pharmacy provided.

***

Sidney couldn't remember ever having felt quite so pissed off. Bar the fighting, the mud and the lice, none of which he much enjoyed, he'd been having quite a cushy little war up until the last couple of weeks. Then it'd all gone tits up. He'd had a nice little number running where they'd been posted before, with a couple of the local Frogs brewing up all sorts, even absinthe, in their back rooms. Filthy stuff it was, but with a hell of a kick. He'd sold it on to the lads at a good profit. That, and the fags, and the occasional set of naughty pictures, had set him up nicely. He'd even had enough left over from what he sent home to Veronica to cop hold of a few tasty titbits for himself - and not always of the edible variety. A quick smile flickered behind

74

his eyes - *Mademoiselle from Armentières* and no mistake! And now here he was, only days away from another bloody show, waiting for some sod that'd been recommended to him as the local fixer, who couldn't be arsed to turn up. Sidney took another swig of his beer. At least the local brew was just about drinkable.

It was well over half an hour past the arranged time when a large, red-faced man came into the cafe. He glanced round, spotted Sidney and came and sat down beside him. The big man waved over to the bar and ordered two beers, one for himself and a second one for Sidney. Sidney shrugged. Why not drink? There was bugger all else to do.

'So, I understand you want to talk to me,' the big man said in heavily accented but perfectly fluent English.

'Yes, that's right,' replied Sidney. 'I'm told we might be able to do business together. Got on well with your mate back down the line, and he said you might be able to set me up in the same sort of way over here. I'm Sidney, by the way,' and he held out his hand to the Frenchman.

'Auguste, I am Auguste,' the man replied, shaking Sidney's hand. 'So what exactly are you looking for?'

'Oh, you know, the usual - fags, booze, saucy pictures. Got anything in that line?'

'Most probably I have. And what do you have for me in return? And don't say money - that's worse than useless to me here at the moment.'

'No problem. What do you need? Boots, ammo, bully beef?'

'Yes, any of that, all of that. What about drugs? Can you get anything in that line?'

'Funny you should say that, I found a nice little supply of this and that just yesterday, but some sodding officer came and kicked me out before I could actually get my hands on the stuff. Morphine and all, I bet they had. Can go back and have another shufti if you make it worth my while.'

'Sounds as though we may be able to do business, mon ami. Let us meet here again in a couple of days, and I'll give you a proper list of requirements and timings.'

'Fair enough. Unless we get our marching orders, I'll be here, day after tomorrow - and expecting some decent stuff ready for my time and trouble.'

'Of course, my friend, of course,' Auguste rose, tapped Sidney reassuringly on the shoulder and made his way out of the café.

Sidney sat on, his elbows on the table, his hands around his beer, comfortable, at ease, just watching people come and go. He was in no rush, and this place was good as any other.

***

In another village, some miles away, the man sat quietly outside the café, nursing a draft beer, as he watched the lanky child coming and going in the street.

The aunt gave him tasks and sent him on errands, which François carried out seriously and with care, going to the grocer's for flour, to the butcher's for a pair of chops or a scrag end of mutton. He would carry the packages carefully, in both hands, as his mother had shown him, and kept his eyes down as he walked, so that he would not trip.

The man noticed that the boy's jacket was too small for him. The child's arms poked from the sleeves, exposing his thin, bony wrists. The trousers, though, were a man's trousers, hacked off raggedly at the ankle, and bunched in the middle, tied with a length of string. It made him look like a scarecrow. The man's lips tightened in displeasure. He rose and walked across to the boy.

'Hello, François, would you like me to help you with that?'

The boy looked up, startled. The man was struck by the clear grey of the child's eyes. François clutched the package more tightly in his hands, holding it against his chest.

'No,' he said, in a light, uncertain voice. 'Tati told me always to carry things myself. She said not to talk to anyone when I was out. I am out now.' François paused, thought to himself, and fell silent. He continued walking.

The man watched as the boy walked away. That was good. But would it be enough?

The man went back and sat outside the little café. Again he approached François as he came back from his errand. Again the boy rebuffed him, but this time less certainly, allowing the man more of a conversation, more contact, more of a way in.

He would give the boy one more chance.

Late in the morning, when the man approached the boy, François smiled at him widely, acknowledging his new friend. He readily handed the small packet of beef over to the man for him to carry.

'When you've finished your chores, François,' said the man, 'Why don't we go fishing? I'm sure you know some good spots you can show me.'

François nodded eagerly.

'After lunch?' he asked in his high clear voice. 'Tati doesn't like me to be in the house in the afternoons when she is sleeping.'

A shadow crossed the man's face, too quickly for the boy to notice.

'After lunch is good. Come and find me at the café and we'll go together.'

The man had no fear of anyone connecting him to the boy. A stranger came, a stranger spoke, a stranger left. And if they did make the connection, what of it? There were millions of men moving from place to place all through the countryside, all through the towns and villages, up and down the roads from Switzerland to the sea. How could they find one amongst so many? And such an ordinary one too.

That afternoon, François marched purposefully up to the man where he sat with his glass of beer. The man stood, swigged down the rest of his drink, and walked with François out of the village, the gangly lad carrying his old fishing rod and bag happily on his shoulder.

***

Fine. There were some things that just had to be done, and now was the time to do them. After all, he'd done it before. And he'd been a whole lot younger then.

Murray sat on the edge of his bed, his bare feet dangling just short of the stone floor, willing himself to lower them just that little bit further, so that he could try to stand. There were only five of the walking wounded left at the CCS - a couple were snoozing, a couple were out in the courtyard having a smoke and a chat, and he was here, marooned on a bed in a barn Somewhere in France. Before he could think about it any more, Murray pushed himself up and off the bed, so that he was standing only slightly uncertainly on the icy cold floor. He paused, inordinately proud of himself. 'I don't suppose they award medals for standing up,' he reflected. He gave what might have been a smile, but his teeth were gritted so tightly it was more of grimace. Hey ho. The muscles in his back, what was left of them, were giving him a high old time, shouting at him to for God's sake get back in bed again. Too bad. He was the one in command, and he was telling them to bally well shut up and do their job properly. Their job was to hold him standing upright, his job, goddamit, was to walk as far as the end of the bed. It wasn't even that far. He was more than halfway down the bed anyway. So. Murray touched his fingers to the coverlet to help himself balance, then cautiously slid his left foot forward. Fine. He was still upright, though bent forward at a strange angle. He slid his right foot forward. Triumph! He'd taken a step! Or, to be more accurate, he'd taken a shuffle. The pain in his back was astonishing, and he felt himself begin to tremble. He had thought he'd walk to the end of the bed and back, but no. He just about had enough resolve to shuffle a step backwards, and then he sank gratefully back onto the bed. Without pausing to think about it, he lifted one leg and then the other back up onto the bed, and laid himself down as best he could, half propped up on his pillows, and simply lay still. He savoured the sense of being supported, the sense of being safe. He felt that something had happened to him, something more than just the physical damage to his back. How he was in the world had been altered in some huge way that he couldn't quite put his finger on. He didn't want to think about it now. It was too much. It was all much too much. He let his eyes close and drifted into a doze.

***

Jack had his hands full. The pharmacist had been thoughtful, generous, and impressively well stocked. The major would be pleased. He stood undecided in front of the entrance to the little café. Should he hurry straight back to the CCS, or would it be alright for him to sit a while, draw breath and drink a long, slow beer? Well, why not? This might be the last opportunity for a bit of R and R for a goodly while, and goodness knows he could do with a rest, and, if the right opportunity arose, with a certain amount of recreation as well. It wouldn't be with any of the women he'd seen hanging around the camp at the far end of the village. He'd seen women enough like that when he was living in Paris, more dismal than disgusting, but certainly nothing to raise his interest. Madeleine, on the other hand, but, well, what chance did he have there? A sickly Englishman who couldn't even lift her child without coughing. No, best not let his thoughts run that way. Celibacy, cigarettes and a long, strong beer. That would do him. Well, it pretty much had to, didn't it?

He made his way to the back of the café, ordering a beer from the bar on the way. He put down his packets on the table, lit up a fag, and leant back to take in the scene.

Most of the tables had soldiers huddled round them, savouring this island of normality, smoking, chatting, drinking. One or two old men as well, locals, enjoying each other's company, and sharing all the gossip. There was one soldier sitting alone at a table at the far side of the room, with a child perched on a chair opposite him. Both looked familiar. Then, with a rush of recognition, Jack realised the child was Alex, and the soldier was the slippery character he'd kicked out of the CCS the day before. Jack leapt to his feet, ready to stride across and seize Alex, then realised that he might frighten the child, and anyway, he really had no idea what was going on. He walked rather less hastily than he might have wished across the room, and nodding at the soldier, sat down at the table next to the little boy.

'Hello, Alex,' he said, looking the child in the eyes. 'What are you up to in a place like this? Does Maman know you're here?'

'Yes,' replied the boy solemnly. 'She told me to come and wait for her here once I got bored with playing. She will come and collect me after she has finished talking to Madame Mardel.'

'And you,' Jack rounded on the soldier. 'Slater, was it? What are you doing with this boy?'

'Nothing, mate, keep your wig on. The lad was looking round for somewhere to sit, and I thought he'd be best off with me until his Mum comes for him. Spitting image of my youngest, he is. Rodney. Miss them something rotten. You got kids?'

Jack was embarrassed. Perhaps he had misjudged this man.

'No, no children, no wife, no best girl, no-one at all, unless you count my sister - and I'm sure she'd not be best pleased to be the subject of conversation in a place like this.'

Sidney smiled. 'War does odd things, don't it? Look,' he went on. 'Why don't you fetch your stuff and come and sit with us? The boy seems to know you, and it'll be better for him to have someone he knows as well as me until his Ma toddles along.'

Jack found himself agreeing with the private. Perhaps he'd been mistaken about him yesterday, and he had only been after something for his blisters? He fetched his beer and the goods he'd picked up from the pharmacist and went to sit with Alex and the soldier.

And that was where Madeleine found them both when she came

80

in looking for Alex. Slightly surprised, she thanked the two men for looking after her son, then the little group broke up, Jack to walk back to the farm with Madeleine and the boy, Sidney to sit quietly over his beer, thinking about his own small family back in Stepney.

**

It had not gone well. At first it had all seemed fine, man and boy walking in silence side by side. Sometimes the boy had said something, and the man had replied, his voice gentle. Sometimes the man had said something, and the boy had replied with quick excitement.

The boy had taken the man to his favourite fishing spot – close to the village and within easy sight of a dozen houses and at least two dozen prying eyes. They had fished there together for a while, catching a few chub, and seeing at least one barbell slip away through the weeds. At length the man had suggested they find somewhere more special, somewhere fewer people would have found, where the fish would be more plentiful. The boy told him that there was one place, a place his cousin had shown him once, but that it was a bit far. He needed to get back before dark or his aunt would be worried.

'What happens when your aunt is worried?' asked the man.

'She gets very cross. Sometimes she used to slap me, but I'm too tall for that now, so she just makes me go to my room without any supper.' François paused, remembering. 'Without breakfast too, sometimes.'

The shadow passed over the man's face again.

'Come, let's find your secret place and catch a big carp for your Aunty. Then she can't be cross.'

François grinned. 'She can't be, can she? She'd like a big carp. I know that there are sometimes huge carp at the place Jeannot showed me.'

Man and boy had strode together across the fields, through a small

81

wood and down to a tributary of the main river. Cousin Jeannot had been right. A pool formed by a curve on the river, and sheltered on both sides by overarching willows, teemed with bream and carp.

They settled side by side on the riverbank and set up their rods. François watched his with close attention. After a while the man rose, as if to fetch something from his bag. He came quietly up behind François and put his hands almost gently around the boy's throat. He had not expected such sudden strength and such a resolute battle by the boy.

Now he sat beside the sprawled, limp body of the man-child. François' face was a deep red, contorted, his tongue thrusting out long and purplish, still wet, from the grimacing lips.

The man looked down at his own hands and arms. There were long scratches from François' finger nails, and bruises starting to swell around his wrists. The man was disappointed in himself. He had fallen prey to assumption and impulse. He thought he had foresworn both. He clearly still had a long way to go. He also had a long way to go with François' body. He was determined that all the little ones should be together, but he had not thought that any of them would be so unwieldy, or so awkward to transport.

The sky darkened as the man sat by the riverbank and thought. He had a number of things to consider. There were the practical problems of transport, of avoiding notice. There were the deeper questions of just how much he could rely on his own judgement at the moment. He wondered, though he would not let himself dwell too far on it just now, as he did not have the space and time to deal with what might arise, but he did wonder whether he had made a mistake with François. It would be a matter of deep regret if that were so.

But now he had to find some way of carrying the child a full day's journey, in a way that would be safe for them both. At length the man smiled. Of course. It was so simple.

But it had taken some arranging. First of all he had to ensure that the secret fishing place would not be disturbed for some time, or that, if it were, nothing untoward would be found. He thought hard, then decided to leave François' fishing tackle set up, with his bag ready beside it, as though the boy had simply wandered off. Should anyone come across it, they would see no reason to think anything unfortunate had happened.

The man carefully packed his own bag, making sure that he had left nothing behind, and that nothing had been spilled and tumbled away in the struggle. He moved everything, including the child, to one side, and carefully went over the ground, using matches to light the area inch by inch until he was sure that everything was in order. The spent matches he wrapped in some leaves and stored in a pocket. He would get rid of them later.

He made his way to where his bag and blanket lay beside the boy. He packed everything up, and slung the bag across his shoulder. He wrapped the boy tightly in the blanket, legs and arms tucked in and held by the thick cloth, then he bent and lifted the awkward bundle. He was heavy now, and beginning to get stiff. Still, he wouldn't have to take him far like this. Soon, there'd be something which would be much better for both of them.

The man trudged across the fields, away from the riverbank and towards a small town which lay over the next ridge of hills. It was rising dawn when he found the place he needed, a small copse about half a mile from the town, where he could lay down his burdens in safety. He made sure everything was hidden with branches and leaves, then moved away to sit with his back to a tree at the edge of the copse. He was tired, and his body was slick with sweat, but the walking had been good. Over the course of the night he had made his peace with himself and with the boy. He realised that, of course, it was not a mistake. That the others would need just such a strong and resolute guardian for the times when he could not be there to watch over them. François had understood, and understood the honour of the post. He had risen to the responsibility with gravity. He had never had such an important task before, and he would fulfil it with all his heart and all his care.

The man waited until the sky had fully lightened so that he could check his appearance. He rolled down his sleeves to cover the scratches. The boy had been mortified when he had seen what he had done, but the man had assured him that he had behaved absolutely properly. In fact, if he had not fought as he had done, the man would never have been able to recognise that he was the stalwart guardian the little ones needed. He was not to fret about it a moment longer.

Once he was sure that he looked presentable, the man strode easily across the field to the little town, and walked along the main street until he found what he was looking for.

Going into the café bar, he felt the eyes of the few inside resting on him with a quiet curiosity which was ready to turn to active hostility in an instant. He walked slowly up to the bar and ordered a beer, and then took it over to one of the small tables near the back of the room. He nodded to the other men sitting around, acknowledging them but not trespassing on their goodwill. He sat quietly, waiting for the advances, the enquiries which would inevitably come.

It wasn't long before an old man ambled over and asked if he could sit at the man's table.

'Passing through?'

'Mmm,' assented the man. 'No place to settle, no reason to settle. Just picking up odd jobs and getting by.'

The old man nodded.

'From over there?' he gestured with his head in the direction of the front line.

The man dipped his head. 'Yes.' He said nothing more. The old man would paint his own picture of what that meant.

'What kind of work you looking for?'

'I've got a job over south, bit of building, bit of carpentry,' said the man. 'Need to pick up wood and bits and pieces, though. Know of anyone with anything round here?' The man made a gesture to the bag he'd laid on the table. 'Got an advance on wages. Can pay.'

He sat back and took a long drink of his beer. The old man's thoughts, and greed, would do the rest.

It wasn't long before the man had acquired six sturdy planks of wood, a bag of nails and a hand cart to transport them. By mid-afternoon he was walking out of the small town, heading south, or at least appearing to do so.

CHAPTER 9

10th November, late night and early morning onwards

It had come to feel almost customary for Olivier and the major to lean together over the farmyard gate leading into the orchard, gazing across at the distant ruined village, smoking their pipes, sharing the silence.

That morning, before the afternoon's events changed everything, Olivier had turned to the major enquiringly.

'Why do you do it?' he asked.

'Why do I do what?' returned the major, summoned back from his daydreams of a small house in Sussex, not too far from the sea. Perhaps Rottingdean?

'Why do you patch these boys up time after time? Why do you help them,' Olivier gestured behind him, encompassing Divisional Headquarters, all the higher ups, all the politicians, in one dismissive sweep of his arm, 'do this?' And he pointed accusingly to the darkened horizon. There was an anger behind his words which startled the little doctor, and he paused to gather his thoughts, wishing to respond to this passionate policeman as seriously and honestly as he could.

'I do it because I can, and if I can, I must.'

He turned so that he was looking Olivier in the eye.

'I don't know whether all this,' and here he too swept his arm wide, as if to include the whole world of the war, 'is right or wrong. I don't know whether it is stupidity, or evil, or pure ill chance, which makes these things happen. But I do know what it means to the poor buggers caught up in it.' The major stopped a moment, surprised to hear the heat with which he spoke. He went on more slowly. 'I do know what munitions and shrapnel and infection can do to a body. If I can,

87

however little, however briefly, mend what they have marred, then that's my sworn duty.' He dropped his eyes and gave a little cough, and fussed with refilling and relighting his pipe, heartily embarrassed to have seemed so emotional.

Olivier looked at the little doctor as he hunched back into himself, puffing to get his pipe going.

'Yes,' he said briefly. 'Of course you must. Of course.'

And the two men settled back into their silence.

***

He had watched as the mourners filed from the churchyard, the priest hurrying to shed his stole so that he could dig in to the funeral tea.

He waited, sad at what he needed to do, but he knew that the one he would be disturbing would understand. It had to be done. He could see no other way.

When the night had fully fallen, and the town had gone to rest, the man stepped from the shelter of the trees where he had been standing watching. With infinite care to make no noise he half pushed, half carried the hand cart along the churchyard path and over to the freshly dug grave. He lifted off the flowers with care and laid them to one side, then worked quickly to dig down through the lightly laid soil. Once the hole was deep enough and wide enough, the man paused. He sat by the side of the opened grave and bowed his head in silent conversation with the poor soul inside the coffin.

It had taken a while to lift the coffin out of the ground, as silently as he could manage, pausing every moment to look round and ensure that he'd not been seen, not been heard. Removing the lid had taken yet more time, and then, there he was, in the darkest, stillest moments of the night, face to face with the dead soldier. A grown man, bearded, his wound not immediately apparent until you looked down and saw he had no legs. The man lifted the dead, maimed soldier out of the coffin with great gentleness, and wrapped him in one of the blankets he'd brought with him. Before covering the soldier's face, the man leaned over and kissed the cold skin of his brow. He laid his hand on the man's head and murmured, 'There, not long now, you'll be at peace again. You've done all you could, and you've helped even more now. You know that, don't you lad?'

Covering the dead man's body with its makeshift shroud, the man lifted him carefully back down into the grave, and then hastily filled it in again, finishing by laying the wreaths and flowers back over the surface. It wasn't perfect, but if you didn't know to look you'd never notice anything.

Laying the coffin on the barrow, the man trod quietly back the way he'd come, out of the graveyard, and over the field.

The sky was growing light as he got back to the small grove where François lay. Carefully, the man wrapped him in his remaining blanket and lifted the stiffened body into the coffin. He laid his bag and all his other belongings on the cart, underneath the coffin, and then roped everything in place. He was tired to the bone, but he knew it was best to start moving now, and put as much distance as he could between them and the small town. In any case, he needed to get François to his new home, and introduce him to his friend.

It was fine at first, through the almost empty roads of the early dawn. Some women on their way to sell whatever produce they had managed to salvage and hoard. Some men on their way to work on whatever land was left to them. Some random flotsam walking up or down, looking for work, for a place to settle, a place to slowly rebuild the tatters of their bodies, of their lives. The man walked on. The sun rose fully and grew warmer, and now the roads were full. Walking men, marching men, horses, carts, guns, all moving with purpose towards their different destinations. The man pushed his cart, head down, occasionally catching glances of sympathy from those who saw the shape on the cart and drew their own conclusions. A father taking his child home to be buried. A companion fulfilling one last difficult task. A workman who'd found a way of making some kind of living out of the tragedies of others. He hunched over and walked on, savouring their sympathy, bowed down by a grief they couldn't guess at.

He had the first precious two, though how he would move the Guardian safely to his new home he was not entirely sure. To be walking like this was good and fine along the road, but he could hardly wheel his barrow, thus laden, into the woods without someone noticing and perhaps questioning. He mulled the problem over as he walked. And then he thought he might have found a solution. Where better to hide a coffin than in a graveyard?

It was night when he arrived at the outskirts of the village, where the old church and the small cemetery stood silent. Beyond the cemetery lay the village. Beyond the village lay the field. Beyond the field lay the wood. And in the wood, he told his charge in a low voice, he would be overseeing all the little ones, to make sure they were not afraid. In the summertime he could show them how to fish, and where to look for rabbits and badgers. As he spoke, his fingers worked at the knots holding the coffin in place on the barrow. He looked around every so often to make sure he was not observed, but here, in deep shadows at the side of the graveyard, it would be hard for an observer, had there been one, to make out anything other than a darker shape among the dark shapes all around.

He shook out the blanket which had lain over the coffin and laid it on the rough grass by the wall right at the edge of the graveyard. Reaching into the barrow, he took his spade and walked slowly along the ranks of the new graves, looking for one that would be right. He didn't want to disturb a grave so fresh the relatives would still be visiting and mourning daily, weekly. Partly because they might notice any changes, but also because he did not want to intrude on their raw grief. No, he wanted a grave that was a few months old, with the harsh edge and tight ritual of that first mourning over, but with the soil still soft. Ah, here. He knelt and carefully set the images and flowers to one side, laying them in exactly the order in which he found them so that he could replace them without making any mistakes. A glance around again, and then he started to dig.

This was going to be harder work than when he had borrowed the coffin for the boy – he had to go several spade's lengths deeper, so that no-one would notice the addition. It took longer than he had hoped, but soon the grave was deep enough for two. Walking quietly back to where the coffin lay on the blanket by the wall, the man lifted out the increasingly limp body of the boy and moved the coffin to one side. He tucked the blanket carefully over the dead child, covering his face so that it would not shine in the moonlight, and telling him of his new friend whom he would meet soon. The empty coffin safely hidden and covered in the grave, the flowers and images replaced, the man went back to where the Guardian lay. He lifted him gently into his arms and walked across the field into the wood.

'You're here now. You're safe now. You can rest easy. And look, there's a playmate for you.' Digging another shallow grave with his hoe, the man laid the lanky body of the child beside the other. Covering the new grave with soil and stones, he sat a while beside the boys, smoking a pipe, and telling them about the other friends they'd soon have staying with them.

***

Yesterday's adventure with setting foot to ground had left Murray both exhausted and exhilarated. As he lay in bed watching the light slowly turning from black to grey to day on the whitewashed wall of the barn, he determined that today he would walk off the ward under his own steam, and greet the day, upright on his own two feet. After the orderly had brought him breakfast, which he had eaten sitting up on the edge of his bed, Murray had asked whether there was anything like a walking stick lying around. The orderly had thought for a bit, and then come back with a nice sturdy walking stick cut, it seemed by the look of it, from walnut. It was slightly too short for Murray, but not so much that he couldn't support himself on it.

With the orderly hovering nervously beside him 'just in case', Murray gingerly put one arm and then the other into his dressing gown, shrugging it awkwardly over his shoulders so as to disturb his back as little as possible. He decided to do without slippers. Better cold feet than sliding and falling on the smooth, time-worn flagstones of the barn. Grasping the walking stick to help him balance, he took the first perilous step away from the safety of his bedside. He was terrified. It was all he could not to turn round and lie back down on the bed. He grinned at the orderly.

'What's that old riddle? What walks on four legs in the morning, two legs at noon, and three legs at dusk?'

The orderly shook his head, slightly uneasy at the hectic gaiety of Murray's tone.

'It was the sphinx, you know, who asked that, and there was some old geezer, can't remember his name, some ancient Ancient Greek who guessed the answer - man. Man it is, who crawls on hands and feet as a child, walks on two legs as a man, and hobbles with a stick when he's old. Well, I must be old then, mustn't I?'

The orderly didn't know what to say, and looked down, embarrassed.

'Yes, I'm an old man, hobbling with my stick like old Mr Hedges the gardener. Still, like Mr Hedges, I can make my way, not swiftly, to be sure, but nonetheless...' And Murray moved, one step after the other, pausing in between to gather himself for the fear and the pain, and setting off again, step by step towards the barn door.

The orderly had followed a few feet behind, not wanting to interfere, but anxious in case the patient should fall.

Once at the doorway, Murray paused and turned towards the orderly, 'Don't suppose you could rustle up a chair for me, could you, old chap? Rather fancy sitting down for a bit just now, eh?'

The orderly hurried away, and was back in next to no time with a sturdy wooden chair.

'Where would you like it, sir?'

'Just there by the wall would be topping,' said Murray, gesturing with his stick. Then slowly, slowly, he crept over the uneven cobbles of the yard until he could grasp the back of the chair and gently ease himself down into it.

***

Madeleine looked out of the kitchen window, keeping an eye out for Olivier and Alex, who had gone to finish off their work in the orchard the moment breakfast was done. She couldn't help noticing the wounded English officer who was sitting in the yard again, white-faced, wearing just a dressing-gown and with bare feet in this chill weather. She looked around, and spotted a pair of Alexandre's clogs sitting in a corner. She hadn't wanted to move them. Having them sitting there made it look as if he'd just popped out and would return at any moment.

She gathered up the quilt off her bed, and, picking up Alexandre's clogs, made her way across the courtyard to the man. She stood before him, slightly awkwardly, and gestured at his bare feet with the clogs.

Murray smiled, a wide, brilliant smile, 'Why thank you, madame, yes, oui, oui, yes,' and lifted his feet so that Madeleine could put the clogs on the ground. They were rather too big for him, and stiff and cold, but a great deal less cold than the cobbles. 'Merci, madame, you are very kind.'

Madeleine gestured questioningly with the quilt - did Murray want it round his shoulders?

'Why yes, oui, merci, thank you so much.'

She placed the quilt around him, then stood silently. Both wanted to speak, neither knew what they could say.

Jack came round the corner of the barn from the sluice room, and saw Madeleine standing there, and then saw Murray sitting with the quilt around him. He went up to them, not sure whether he was feeling glad that he had an opportunity to speak to Madeleine, or sorry that she had clearly been looking after Murray.

'Hello, old man,' he nodded to Murray. 'Did you walk all the way out here under your own steam?'

'Well, me and my trusty walking stick,' replied Murray, holding up the stick for Jack to see. 'Hey, old chap, could you say to Madame how grateful I am for the quilt and clogs? My French is, to say the least, ropey.'

'Of course,' said Jack, and, turning to Madeleine, he told her how grateful Murray was to her for keeping him warm. 'Tell me, madame,' he went on. 'Is there any news of your friend's little boy?'

Madeleine shook her head sadly. 'No, nothing, and there is word of another boy missing from over towards Villers, but I don't how true that is. You know how rumours fly around at the moment.'

'Madame, I am so sorry,' said Jack warmly.

Murray picked up his tone. 'What is it? Is something the matter?'

Jack asked Madeleine if it would be alright if he told Murray what they had been talking about.

'Of course,' she shrugged. 'I must get back and see to lunch. Perhaps you could be so kind as to bring back the quilt and clogs when monsieur has finished with them?'

'With pleasure, madame,' Jack smiled, happy to have a reason to see Madeleine again later in the day.

***

Murray had been shocked by what Jack had told him - one, perhaps two small boys missing, and no-one seeming prepared to do anything about it.

Jack had tried to explain the situation as far as he'd been able to piece it together. 'It seems the police can't do anything because we're in a military zone, and the MPs can't do anything because the little boy and his mother are civilians. Madeleine, Madame Blanchard, and the other women in the village have been doing what they can, but Madame Mardel, Paul's mother, has been going out of her mind. It's been over a week now, and no sign of him. And now it seems another little lad has disappeared as well, from a village just a few miles away. It's all very rum.'

Murray felt something break open inside him. He was flooded with passionate feeling. He had no idea what that feeling was - was it anger? Anguish? Grief? Compassion? He just knew that he had been feeling nothing for days, months, years on end, and now he felt filled with a burning desire to act - how, why, in what direction, to what end, none of that mattered. What mattered was doing something, now, this minute.

'More than just rum, I'd say!' Murray's cry startled Jack. 'It's diabolical! Here these women are, the enemy in front of them, soldiers all around them, they're surrounded by guns and gas and bombs, and you're telling me there's no one here who can help them keep their children safe? Well, bugger that!' And he made to stand up, only to be held fast by the appalling agony that flared along his spine. He gripped the seat of the chair, white-faced.

'Easy, easy,' Jack leant over him, muttering gentle sounds, trying to soothe the wounded man, to relieve the pain he saw.

Jack settled the quilt back around Murray's shoulders, and stood at his side, wondering what he should do next.

He had an idea that the best thing for the patient would be to get back to bed, and to rest for a good long while. But no sooner had Jack had the thought than he wondered whether that wasn't being purely self-serving on his own part - tuck the lieutenant away on the ward, and take the quilt and clogs back to Madame. Perhaps sit by her fire. Perhaps talk with her a little.

He almost seemed to shake himself. Deliberately he turned to Murray, 'What would you like to do, old man? You seem pretty shaken up.'

'I am angry, that's what I am,' Murray replied. 'I am utterly fucking furious. I hate where we are, I hate being in pain, I hate not being with my men, I hate being so bloody fucking useless, and I hate that there seems to be no way to help these women whose children are missing.'

'You're right, old man, and of course, there must be a way. Why don't you go back to bed for a while and get your strength up, and I'll see if I can get everyone together for a bit of a chat this afternoon to get a proper idea of what's what, and to see what, if anything, we can possibly do to help.'

Jack helped Murray to his feet and half supported him back along the ward and into his bed.

'I'll get her things back to Madame and set up a time when we can all put out heads together.'

Murray lay back on the cold sheet, his head resting on the pillow, his eyes closed.

'Thanks, old man. I'll just wait here then,' and it almost seemed for a moment as though he smiled.

***

Madeleine's quilt and clogs in hand, Jack went in search of the major. He explained what Madame had told him, and Murray's reaction. 'Is there anything we can do to help, sir, do you think? It seems wrong that children should go missing and that no one should be lifting a finger to do anything about it.'

The major smiled at his earnest, tender-hearted orderly.

'You're right, lad. It is wrong. But whether it's a wrong that we're in any position to put right I really don't know. Why don't we see if all of us together, you, the lieutenant, Madame, the ex-policeman and me, can think of something.'

'Ex-policeman, sir?' asked Jack, puzzled.

'Why, yes indeed.' The major smiled. ' It seems Olivier the handy-man is a bit of a dark horse. He used to be some sort of high panjan-drum in the police down in Lyons, a detective, I believe. He's just the very man to give us the right advice. Go and see if you can find him, and see if you can arrange with Madame for us all to meet together in her kitchen, if she's agreeable, at, say five this afternoon. Let me know as soon as you can, there's a good lad.'

Jack gave his shadow salute, and made his way across the yard to the farmhouse.

He wondered whether Madeleine would be there, and what she would think of this sorry bunch of the aged and the ailing wanting to come to the rescue of her friends.

***

Michel, Michel Dubois. He was the next.

He had watched the little boy for days, and watched her too. Seen how she shooed Michel out of the house first thing in the morning and only called him to bed as the sun was sinking. Watched through the window as she sat at the table in the small kitchen, reading a book and drinking first coffee, then wine as the day progressed.

She was no fit guide for the child. The others would look after him and keep him safe.

***

Madeleine lifted her head from her sewing when she heard the qui-et tapping at the door. No one she knew knocked quite so quietly. Puzzled, she tucked her needle safely into the cloth, and rose to open the door. The pale English nurse was standing outside, holding her quilt and Alexandre's clogs. He smiled.

'Madame, may I come in a moment? As well as returning your

things, I wonder if I might have a word?'

Madeleine took the quilt and clogs from him, and gestured for him to enter. The two stood awkwardly for a moment, until Madeleine invited Jack to sit opposite her beside the fire. She took up her sewing, and continued turning one of Alexandre's big working shirts into a little shirt for their son.

'Madame, it's about the missing children.' Madeleine stopped sewing and gazed steadily at the Englishman.

'What of them?' Her voice was clipped and tight. Was she afraid he had bad news for her?

'It's nothing to concern you, madame,' Jack hastened to reassure her. 'It's just that we - that is my commanding officer and the wounded soldier, Lieutenant Coverdale, and myself - were wondering whether there was anything we could do to help. And perhaps your handyman, Monsieur Olivier is it, too? If we put our heads together, perhaps we might be able to find some clue as to what has happened to Madame Mardel's son and to the other missing boy. What do you think?'

'But how? What can you all do when the police and the army say they can't do anything?'

'Indeed, I am not sure, madame, what we can do, but between us, with you as well, of course, we might get some idea about where to look for the boys, and bring them home to their mothers. Even if they have perished lost on the roads, then surely it is better their mothers know, and have a body to bury and grieve over, rather than this is awful uncertainty? Will you let us at least try, madame? A meeting here this evening, with all five of us sharing what we know, could we do that, do you think? Who knows what might come of it? Perhaps nothing, but then again, perhaps something.'

Jack paused, and sat quietly, with eager eyes, while Madeleine pondered.

'I cannot see that it will do harm, and perhaps it may do good, as you have said. Olivier and Alex are in the orchard. When they return,

I will ask Olivier what he thinks. If he agrees, then by all means let us meet early this evening, after Alex is in bed. Seven thirty would be a good time. I'll send Alex across later to let you know whether Olivier agrees, and perhaps I'll see you again this evening.'

She rose and laid aside her sewing, keeping her eyes cast down for a moment before raising them to look straight at Jack, a questioning, troubled look.

Jack too stood and went to the door.

'Thank you, madame, I'll wait to hear from the little lad.'

***

Olivier had thought it worth trying, and so now the four men were seated around the old oak table in the farmhouse, while Madeleine kept to her place by the fire, giving such information as she had when asked, but otherwise sewing quietly and listening intently as the men sought to make such sense as they could out of the matter. Every so often Jack would summarise what they had been discussing for her in his immaculate Parisian French. Otherwise they spoke in English, while Madeleine listened to the tones of their voices, watched their hands, their shoulders, and the anxiety or anger they expressed.

Olivier gestured towards the paper on which he'd been making notes.

'This is good. We know something. We can see some things. But there is more, much more, we need to find out if we are to understand what is happening here.'

Jack lifted his head from his hands. His pale face shone in the dark room.

'Understand it, and restore these children to their mothers.'

There was a silence.

Suddenly it seemed as though something black and unrelenting had entered the room and stood beside them.

99

Murray shook himself, and reached for the paper he'd been writing on.

'Well, then, we need a plan.'

The small group were sitting together around the solid oak table in Madeleine's kitchen.

'From what we know so far, it seems that we have two boys who have gone missing, one who is a child in years, one with the understanding of a small child.' Olivier spoke slowly and deliberately. 'What else do we know?

'They lived locally, but not so close to each other that they were likely to know each other. That will be something to follow up on, though. Did they know each other? Are they colluding together in some way, off on what they see as some sort of adventure?

'Neither of them seems to have left any kind of clue as to where they went or why, nor to have taken anything with them - toys, food, clothing - when they disappeared. But again, that is something that will need checking.

'So, if they're not off on some sort of adventure together, and I honestly don't believe they are, although I will make enquiries to find out for sure, but, assuming they're not,' Olivier paused for a moment and looked around at the small group as they sat listening to him intently, 'assuming they're not, that leaves us with just two possibilities.

'Either this is just a pair of random accidents, individual tragedies with only bad luck and the chaos of war linking them together, or else there is something far more sinister going on.

'For myself, I have no great belief in coincidence. One small boy getting lost - a common enough occurrence. Two young boys disappearing off the face of the earth with no clue as to what has happened to them? That is not mischance. That, I am very much afraid, means mischief.'

Madeleine looked anxiously across at the retired policeman. 'Sinister, you said sinister. What do you mean? Who could possibly want to harm small children?'

Olivier strode over to her and crouched down beside her chair so that he was looking her directly in the eye. 'Madeleine, it may just be some lunatic, with no reason we could understand behind his actions. I fear though, given that we are speaking of at least two children, that there is something much worse afoot.'

The major looked earnestly across at Olivier. 'I fear you may be right. Not a madman, but a gang.'

'A gang, but what, why?' Madeleine's fear and confusion were obvious. 'What would a gang want with little boys?'

'Probably not for themselves, Madeleine,' Olivier explained gently. 'But as something to sell.'

'To sell? But why? To whom? For what? I don't understand!'

Olivier looked at her earnestly, and then stood, moving away from her back to his chair.

'And best you don't, my dear. Best you don't.'

***

Dusk had been falling when the man had leant with the small boy, admiring the hutch which the little lad had cobbled together for the rabbit he had rescued.

'It was caught in a trap and its leg was hurt but I got it out and brought it home and cleaned it and fed it leaves and gave it lots of water. It was just a kit, really, and very scared, but I talked to it, and made it somewhere safe, and now it's my friend. See?' The small boy grinned up at the man as the rabbit hopped over to them and squatted happily beside the little boy to have his head scratched.

The man said nothing, but reached over into the hutch and stroked the rabbit as well. Such soft fur, so tame. Such a gentle, loving lad. The man looked around him. He knew the mother was asleep, sprawled over the kitchen table, wine glass in hand. He could see no one else in the gathering gloom. He put his arm around the little boy's slight shoulders and rested his other hand on top of the boy's tangled hair. Then, with a quick twist of his strong wrists, he broke the boy's neck.

He laid him gently against his chest, the head lolling against his shoulder, then he reached in and picked up the rabbit, tucking it firmly down inside his jacket, where it snuggled down in the warm and seemed to go to sleep. It was a sweet, trusting creature, and, as the boy had said, his friend. It wouldn't be fair to separate them.

CHAPTER 10

11ᵗʰ November, early morning onwards

Jack felt restless. Until the push actually began, there wasn't a great deal more he could do at the CCS. The beds had been stripped, the linen and blankets stacked, the bandages wound. The operating theatre was freshly painted and as spotlessly clean as carbolic and several scrubbings could make it. The drugs were sorted, labelled, stacked and safely stored under lock and key. Murray was the only patient left, and as soon as he could walk without a stick he'd be going back to his unit.

He walked across the yard to the farmhouse and knocked on the major's office door.

'Yes,' came the cry. 'Come in, come in.'

'Sir,' said Jack, stepping into the room. 'Might I take a stroll into the village if there's nothing urgent you'd like me to do here? I feel at a bit of a loose end, and I thought a walk might do me good.'

'Of course, of course, excellent idea, Jack. If you see any bread or rolls in the baker's while you're down that way, they'd be most appreciated,' and he tossed a two franc piece across the desk to Jack.

Catching the coin, Jack turned on his heel and left. 'Be back by lunchtime, sir,' he called over his shoulder.

***

Sidney was feeling increasingly uneasy. There was a tension in the air, a stifling sense of something not quite happening. There were more men posted in and around the village than there had ever been before. More men, more munitions, more officers, more sodding

MPs. He had got together as much as he could of what Auguste had asked for, and now he wanted rid, sharpish.

He made his way in what he hoped appeared to be a relaxed saunter along the street to the little cafe. With his luck Auguste wouldn't turn up until after he had to go back on duty, but it was worth a try. Anything was worth a try to get the goods out from where he'd stored them and well away from any connection to him. It was all getting a bit too dodgy for his taste. Sidney sat in the café, nursing a beer, his back to the wall and his eyes constantly darting between the door and his pocket watch. The last thing he needed at the moment was to be put on a charge.

Men came in and men went out. Young men in uniform striding purposefully, old men in dusty jackets, shuffling, heads down. None of them was Auguste.

Sidney's fingers tapped and tapped on the table. He couldn't be doing with this. He really fucking couldn't be doing with this. With an exasperated sigh he swigged back the last of his beer, pushed back his chair and strode out of the cafe - and ran straight into Auguste, making his way towards the door.

'Where the fuck have you been?' Sidney's voice was low but urgent. 'I've been waiting for you here all fucking morning. I've got the goods for you. Where shall we make the swap?'

Neither man, intent on getting their business done and then being rid of each other, noticed Jack watching them.

He had been walking down the street, thinking of Madeleine and little Alex, of the boys who had gone missing, of what Olivier and the major had been speaking about the previous night, and then he'd glanced towards the café and seen that slimy soldier run slap bang into the fat Frenchman. The Frog (and why wasn't the bugger in uniform?) didn't seem upset. In fact, the two seemed to be having quite the conversation, heads together. Jack stepped quietly closer to see if he could overhear what they were saying without being noticed. Walking as slowly as he could, he slipped past them into the café.

'Tonight...' He'd heard. 'They're not going to be easy to transport...' 'You're going to be getting enough, God knows. Don't make such a fuss...'

Jack found himself a seat and ordered a coffee. Did it mean what he feared it meant, and if it did, what should he do, considering all he had heard?

Some he understood - after all, the soldier was a type he knew of old, from home and from South Africa. A chancer, a fly boy - not bad, but not good either. He sipped his coffee and mulled over how he would phrase it if he was writing it up for his old newspaper - 'Private Slater, morally unaligned'. Jack had a certain sympathy for the soldier, for what on earth could all this mess mean to him? Why not do all he could to profit from this chaos as long as he was able? But what was it he was doing, and at whose cost? Could he really be trafficking in small boys for profit? Jack found it hard to believe, even of someone as equivocal as Slater.

But he could easily believe it of the Frenchman. He looked as though he was capable of anything, and had done most things. Kidnapping children and selling them on? Yes, Jack could believe it of him. But believing it of him was a far cry from proving it. And, as Olivier had made clear, intuition and speculation counted for nothing when bringing criminals to book.

He needed to find proof.

Pushing himself up from the table, he made his way out of the café and, hands thrust deep in his pockets, turned his face towards the CCS. As he walked, he turned over the problem again and again in his head. He knew the language, he knew something about the place, he knew a few of the people. There must be a way in for him there somewhere.

***

His morning tasks done, Olivier sat for a while at the table in Madeleine's kitchen, the notes which Murray had made and the notes he himself had been making spread out before him across the time-worn oak. Two boys missing, now perhaps a third. There seemed to be the beginnings of a pattern, but really there was far too little to go on. Just anecdotes, not evidence. It was evidence he needed. Collecting all the pieces of paper together, he folded them carefully and, tucking them into an inside pocket, stepped out into the farmyard. Madeleine was sweeping out the cowshed. Olivier leaned round the door.

'Madeleine, I'm just going to walk up into the village and have a quick word with Mme Mardel, if she's up to it. Is there anything you'd like me to get for you while I'm there?'

Madeleine looked up and swept a stray hair from where it dangled across her eyes.

'No, that's fine, thank you. Just give her my greetings,' and she bent back to her brush.

The retired policeman felt an unfamiliar bounce in his step. Missing children and he was feeling eager, energised. What kind of a monster was he? He upbraided himself, but then thought perhaps it wasn't the fact that the children had gone missing that made him feel more alert, but the fact that he might be able to use his skills to find them. He hadn't realised how much he had been vegetating here in this small village, even with all the misery and chaos of the war all around him. Looking after his mother as she had been dying, helping out Madeleine on the farm, doing whatever he could for the elderly, the widowed, the abandoned stranded here while the battles broke in waves across their land, it was good, it was necessary, but it wasn't enough. Now he had the chance to apply all the knowledge and experience he had garnered during his long career, and to do something no one else could, find out what had happened to these little boys, and if there was a man's hand behind their disappearance - and, if there was, to track that man down and catch the bastard.

As he strode along, Olivier organised in his mind the questions he needed to ask Mme Mardel, and thought through what he felt would be the best way to approach the desperately anxious, grieving woman.

Arriving at her door, he knocked firmly. He almost smiled to himself when he heard he had not knocked the quiet, questioning knock of a neighbour, but the imperious, confident knock of a policeman.

Mme Mardel opened the door, her face pale, her eyes dark, her lips tight, her features even more sunken and drawn than usual.

'Yes? What do you want? There's nothing for you here,' and she went to close the door again.

In an almost instinctive gesture, Olivier wedged his foot in the doorway to prevent her shutting him out. All his carefully planned words of care and commiseration flew from his head. This woman was angry.

'What is it you want? Why have you come? Is there not enough trouble in the world? Do you have to bring your miseries to my door?'

'Madame, please, madame.' Olivier held both hands up. 'I bring no troubles to your door. Indeed, I hope to bring you help. Forgive me if I intrude, but I understand from Mme Blanchard that your son Paul has gone missing. I was wondering whether you might allow me to help find him. I used to be a policeman until just a few years ago, and I thought that, perhaps...'

Madame Mardel held up her hand.

'I know Mme Blanchard means well,' she interrupted forcefully, 'but I don't want or need your help, however grand you think you are. If the boy's gone he's gone, just like his father before him. I have Angelique and Marianne, they're both good girls and work hard. That boy was nothing but trouble. Fidgeting and filthy most of the time. If he comes back, well and good, if not, well no loss, I say, and more to go round for the rest of us.'

She crossed her arms and stood in the doorway, her mouth even more tightly clenched shut, her features even greyer and sharper, a hatchet of a woman.

'Madame,' Olivier backed away from the door. 'I certainly don't mean to disturb you, and of course, you know what's best.'

Her steely glare suggested that Madame Mardel was not to be won over by soft words. Olivier drew himself up.

'I still believe you may be able to help.' His tone was sterner now. 'You see, there is one, perhaps two other boys as well as Paul who have gone missing. It may be more than just a silly boy getting up to mischief. It may be...'

He saw Madame Mardel flinch as though he had struck her. She drew a harsh breath, then shut her lips even more tightly. Olivier saw her knuckles whiten as her hands gripped her elbows, holding herself rigidly upright in the doorway.

Was it terror for her son or terror for herself which had seized her?

Olivier slowed his words, and spoke infinitely gently.

'Madame, perhaps if I might just come in a moment? Could we speak a little about when you last saw Paul, what he was doing, what he was wearing, where he was playing?' Olivier edged forward, and Madame Mardel stepped back and gestured awkwardly for him to come inside the tiny cottage. He stepped over the threshold.

'Thank you, madame. Even the smallest detail, however slight, however trivial-seeming, may be of help.'

Slowly Madame Mardel sank into a wooden armchair which sat on the left-hand side of the empty fireplace. Its twin stood opposite on the other side, and Olivier moved hesitantly towards it. He looked enquiringly at Madame until she waved wearily towards the chair, in silent acceptance that he should sit and ask his questions.

Olivier sat on the very edge of the chair, and, leaning forward, looked earnestly at this complicated, closed woman.

'Tell me about Paul,' he asked quietly.

Madame Mardel gazed down at her hands, clenched tightly together in her lap.

'What is there to say? He was born too early - the curé came and baptised him, and gave him extreme unction the very afternoon he was born. No one expected him to last the night. But last he did. That night, and the next, and the next. He was a sickly, whining baby, and a sickly whining child. He never played with the other boys, he never joined in with his sisters, he was always just there, hanging around outside the house, picking and poking at things. Once he brought in a rat he wanted to keep as a pet. I soon put an end to that. I killed it with the coal shovel and made him bury it out by the privy. He had no sense, that one, and every winter he was ill. He'd have cost me a fortune at the pharmacy if he'd had his way. And now he's gone. I've done my best to look for him, but there's nor hide nor hair of him to be found. What am I supposed to do, monsieur?' She glared across at Olivier. 'I have two daughters to clothe and feed. The gendarmes will do nothing, the soldiers are worse than useless. The boy wouldn't have the wit or the strength to last this long out in the cold on his own. No, he's dead, monsieur. Got lost like the loon he is, or fallen into a ditch somewhere. Nothing more to be done.' She slapped her hands on her knees and stood. She wanted this conversation over.

Olivier stood as well. 'Thank you, madame. I am sorry you have had so much to cope with, and then this,' he opened his hands out to indicate the loss of the child. 'Could you just tell me, do you think, the last time you saw your son?' He had noticed that the mother had never spoken the boy's name, and so avoided doing so himself.

'Ten days ago, it was,' she replied in a dull monotone. 'He said he was going fishing!' She snorted derisively. 'He didn't even have a rod!'

'Where would he have gone to fish, madame?'

'Lord, I don't know! Up by the stream probably, maybe in the canal. There was no knowing with him. Could have been anywhere or nowhere.'

She shrugged and marched briskly to the door.

'Now, monsieur, I have a lot to do, and no more time to sit gossiping. I'll thank you to go now.'

And so Olivier found himself in short order out in the street again, the door firmly shut against him.

Not an easy woman, he mused. Not an easy life, of course, but still, something odd there. Unfeeling? Or maybe feeling too much? He shrugged and pondered what he should do next. While he was here he might as well go and have a look along the river bank and down by the canal. Perhaps he might find some sort of clue as to where little Paul had got to, something the flinty Mme Mardel might have missed.

***

Three now were safe. The man sat with them in the woods. If he was still enough, he could almost hear them chatting and playing together. Michel would be showing them his rabbit. He glanced across to the little cage he'd put together for the rabbit. It was nibbling away happily at the tough old dandelion leaves and the few handfuls of dry grass he'd gathered for it. Michel would be glad to have it there for them all to play with.

Paul, François, Michel. He smiled fondly. Such good boys.

But he was anxious. There was too much going on out there. They thought he couldn't see, but he knew. Oh yes, he knew. He could scent their bloody intentions, their vile purposes, their lust. He had seen the men marching up. He had seen the guns. They thought they were hidden with their nets and scattered bits of leaf. Not hidden from him. And he had seen the new monsters, belching smoke as they were herded into their hiding places. So much that was happening, and so much still for him to do. He felt the panic rise in him. No, no. He still had more to look after. He recited their names to himself, first under his breath, and then aloud, so that the little ones could hear, and know they would soon have more friends to play with and look after.

***

Olivier had walked along the canal side for half a mile or so, until he was stopped from going any further, politely but firmly, by a pair of English soldiers who had clearly been posted there to prevent anyone proceeding past that point. Beyond them he could just make out large awkward shapes draped over with camouflage netting. His curiosity was outweighed by his caution, and he turned back. Pausing a moment, he stood and gazed into the dull dark waters of the canal. When had this canal been dug from the heavy land? 17th century? 18th century? And all to make rich men richer, moving barge-loads of grain and goods from field and factory to merchants' warehouses. Goods the men who dug the canals with spade and mattock could only wonder at. There were times when the elderly policeman felt that nothing changed at all over the generations. The rich did what they wanted, and the poor did what they had to. Bah! He shrugged his shoulders in irritation at the direction his thoughts were taking. Fatalistic nonsense. As if a man could not choose how he lived his life. Of course, some choices were more difficult than others, some lives harder to live, but to live well or ill, to be brutal or kind, that was always a choice that could and must be made. He was convinced, in his heart of hearts, that these missing boys were being dealt with brutally. He was determined to get to the bottom of what was happening, and to stop it.

He strode on, thinking over what he had learned so far to try and make some kind of sense of it. Two boys just gone from one moment to the next. They didn't know each other, they weren't friends, they weren't even from the same villages, so what, indeed, did they have in common? Not their ages. The general locality? A thought brought Olivier to a full stop. They knew of these two boys almost by chance, through the gossip of the women in the village and beyond. But just how many small boys were actually missing? Just how far afield did this web stretch? How could they find out?

He found himself back at the edge of the village, having found no trace of Paul Mardel.

He reached into his pockets for his pipe and tobacco, stuffing the bowl with deft fingers as he strode through the village and back to the farm. He clenched the pipe firmly between his teeth, not bothering to light it, striding ever faster as his anger and frustration built. There was a crime here - he knew it, he could feel it, he could smell it. But what could he do about it? Here he was, an old man, retired, wandering about in the middle of a war zone. Madame Mardel had tried the police, and they'd told her they couldn't do anything. She'd tried the army, and they'd shrugged her off. At the very best, she was an irrelevancy to them. But her child was still missing. And now, so was this other boy. If he'd been down in Lyons still, of course, he could have mobilised his team and got them digging into everything. But here he was, on his own, out of touch, cut off. And furious.

***

Jack and Olivier had returned to the farm at almost the same time, both silent and preoccupied. Each man busied himself with the tasks that needed doing, Olivier around the farm, Jack around the Clearing Station.

It was dusk when the two men were drawn together. Olivier had been leaning on the gate, deep in thought, though to what good effect he had no idea. Jack stepped quietly across the yard and stopped, tentatively, by the older man's side.

'Might I speak with you a moment, monsieur?'

'Of course, of course.' Olivier turned towards the younger man, noting his pallor and his anxious expression. 'There's something bothering you?'

'Well, yes, yes there is. But whether it's anything or nothing, I really have no idea. ' Jack paused. 'You have so much more experience of these things, sir. I'd very much value your opinion.'

Jack told the older man all about the conversation he had overheard between the shady English soldier and the fat Frenchman.

'Do you think there could be anything in it, sir? Do you think they might have been talking about the missing boys?'

Olivier hesitated.

'Let me ask you a few questions before I answer yours. First of all, tell me more about this Frenchman who was talking to your soldier. Do you think he was local?'

'Well, yes, I think so. He was speaking in the local accent, and he looked, oh, I don't know, at home, standing chatting outside the café.'

'Can you describe him to me?'

'He was tall, taller than I am, and solidly built, with quite a belly on him. White hair slicked back and a thick moustache a bit like General Kitchener's.'

Olivier had a feeling he might know who this man might be. If he was right, it wasn't good news at all.

Jack looked at him anxiously.

'Could it be something about the boys, do you think? Do you think they're in cahoots together?'

'If the man you described is the man I think it is, then they're almost certainly in cahoots, as you call it. But what they're in cahoots about, well, we really don't have enough to go on, do we?'

'But the boys - What do you think we should do? We can't just let it go, can we?'

Jack's cheeks were flushed, his eyes wide.

'No, of course not,' replied Olivier thoughtfully. 'But we need to know more. Will you be going back into the village tomorrow, do you think?'

'I can certainly try, if the major doesn't need me for anything.'

Olivier hesitated. He wanted to give Jack something to do, something that would channel this feverish energy and curb his anxiety, without putting him at risk. If the Frenchman Jack had described was indeed who he thought it was, he was a man, Olivier believed, capable of anything.

'Well, why don't you go and just sit quietly in the café with a beer, and see what you can hear and then report back to me tomorrow evening?'

'Yes, yes, I can do that. Of course, I can do that.'

Jack thanked the old policeman and went back across to the ward, his back straighter, a sense of purpose in his step.

Olivier looked after him, his eyes shadowed with worry. He hoped he hadn't done something stupid.

CHAPTER 11

12th November, dawn onwards

12th November, dawn onwards

He hadn't been sure about the next one for quite a while. Jean-Marie Leclerc. Brown haired, brown eyed, the youngest child of eight – all the others, all brothers, either working in reserved occupations or in the army. Jean-Marie was only four years old - must have been a bit of a surprise for everyone concerned. Certainly not part of the family plan. The dad had died just before the war (black lung from the mines). Jean-Marie pretty much brought himself up, wearing his brothers' cast-offs, being overseen by his tiny, wizened, ineffective grandmother, while mother worked in the local bar, cleaning and serving behind the bar on occasion.

He watched. He hesitated. The mother seemed to be doing her best. But the grandmother, she was scarcely coping – hardly seemed aware the boy was there most of the time. No, it needed to be done. The little one needed to be with his friends. They'd make sure he was alright.

***

It was late morning before Jack could get away from the CCS. Every moment since he'd woken up he had been replaying the snippets of the conversation he had overheard again and again in his head. What were the two men talking about? What was being delivered? Olivier was right. He had to find out more, and the café was the best place to start.

He strode down the road towards the village. He felt more alive than he had for a long time. He was, after all, he realised, first and foremost a journalist, and he felt in his blood, however thin, however feverish it might be, that he had stumbled on to a real story here. Something shabby, something hidden was going on. And if it was to do with the missing boys, he was determined to find out just what was happening, and drag the whole filthy mess into the light of day. He hadn't felt so fired up, so full of purpose since he'd been in South Africa. He was determined that he was going to dig up that slimy little private out from whatever rock he was hiding under, take him somewhere quiet and force the truth out of him.

***

Sidney sighed with relief. The handover had gone well, he'd got a nice fat stash of postcards of pleasantly plump little pigeons in the altogether, as well some good strong bottles of grog and a crate of Woodbines that had just happened to fall off the back of a lorry right at that Frenchman's feet. A rum sort he was, that Frog. Sidney was more than glad to have got the deal sorted and to be shot of him. He didn't think he'd be doing business with him again.

Tonight he'd start spreading cheer around the camp. A regular fucking Father Christmas he'd be. But just now, with everything squared away, he was going to treat himself to a beer or three, and just watch the world go by.

***

Jack didn't see him at first, wedged as he was up against the back wall of the café, one glass almost empty in front of him, another two already drained lined up on the table, and a smug expression on his skinny runt's face. Should he go straight up to him and challenge him? No, best not. He realised he needed to sit and think a bit, and come up with a proper plan of action. The private didn't look as if he was going anywhere in a hurry. Jack looked around and found a seat on its own tucked away near the front. He could see the door from there. He couldn't see the private, but, more importantly, the private couldn't see him. Marianne, the bar owner's wide-hipped wife, shuffled over and plonked a glass of draft in front of him, unasked. Jack nodded absently in thanks and settled back to think. Gradually an idea took shape. He turned his chair slightly so that he could keep an eye on the jumbled pathway of chairs and tables that led from the back of the café to the door, and then settled back to wait. Won't you come into my parlour? said the spider to the fly.

***

At first the man had been angry with himself. He'd found the boy playing in the street as usual, the door to the cottage ajar behind him, and the old lady just visible in the dim room, nodding over some sewing which had fallen into her lap from her sleeping fingers. He'd knelt beside the boy and chatted to him, telling him about the magical place in the woods where he could play with his friends all day long. He told him about Michel's rabbit, with its silky ears and soft wet nose. Jean-Marie had listened wide-eyed. He described the dappled wood, the small wild creatures who led their lives there, peacefully, far from harm. Would Jean-Marie like to go there, he'd asked. The child had hesitated. Could he really? Wouldn't the other children mind? No, no, he'd said, they'd love to meet him and to have another playmate to share their games. Jean-Marie had leapt to his feet, eager to go with him, longing to meet these new friends. "I'll just go and tell Mami," he'd said, hurling himself towards the cottage door. He'd had no choice but to bundle the boy up in his arms, a hand tight over his mouth, and hurry him over the ditch and away, rushing towards the wood.

And all that quiet happiness, all that eager joy was gone. Jean-Marie stiff and squirming in his arms, kicking and squeaking and trying to cry out.

It was no good. The boy had to be quiet. He'd frighten the others

117

carrying on like this. And so he'd stopped at the edge of the wood and, holding the little wriggling infant under one arm, he'd pulled his hunting knife out of the sheath on his belt, and cut the child's throat. It was a good knife and a deep cut, and the child was silenced, but it wasn't what he'd wanted at all. The boy had been so happy, and then he'd gone and spoiled it. He'd laid the little body down limp on the cold grass. They were both drenched in blood. What would the others think of all this mess? It wasn't right, it wasn't what he'd meant at all. Sinking down beside the child, he put his head in his hands. How had it gone so wrong?

***

Jack had scarcely touched his beer. He was sitting very still. At first glance you'd have thought him a rather quiet young man, relaxing. A longer look might have revealed the tapping of Jack's finger against the glass, and the way his eyes kept darting to the area just before the café door. And if you'd happened to brush against him as you went to find a table, you would have felt him quivering with tension.

He'd been sitting there for nearly an hour when he saw Sidney slouch his way through the crowded bar towards the door. He looked glassy-eyed and unsteady on his feet. So much the better. Jack stood up quietly, laid a few coins on the table to pay for his drink, and followed the drunken soldier into the street.

Jack had been in two minds as to how to approach the private, but seeing him like this, swaying clumsily along, staying close to the walls to help him balance, Jack knew precisely what to do. Slightly quickening his stride, he drew up beside the soldier.

"You alright, private?" he asked, sounding concerned but not too friendly.

Sidney reeled to see that bloody medic suddenly looming up beside him.

"Yes, sir. Thank you, sir. All good, sir." He tried saluting, but almost overbalanced.

"There, there," said Jack. "Probably best if I see you back to camp, don't you think?" And putting his arm under the soldier's elbow, he led him along the street, and then round a corner, and another, and another, until the private was thoroughly bewildered and completely lost.

"'S not the way to the camp," he protested, pulling his arm away from Jack's insistent hand and looking round blearily.

They were in a small yard full of rusting odds and ends, high blank walls on three sides.

"No," replied Jack. "It's not the way to the camp, but it is a nice quiet place for a chat, don't you think?" And he pushed Sidney back so that he tottered and fell against an old plough-share left half-leaning against the wall. "Why don't you sit down, old chap, and take a breather? Here, have a fag." Jack offered his crumpled packet of Woodbines to the soldier, who sat down heavily and took a cigarette.

"What's this all about, then? What d'ya want?"

"What I want, private, is the truth."

***

The major laid down his pen and flexed his fingers. He felt as if he'd been writing and responding, noting and listing, for half his life. And he'd barely made a beginning. If the Hun didn't do for him, the bloody paperwork would. He sighed, stretched and screwed the top onto his fountain pen. He needed a breather. And anyway, he'd best go and see how things were moving along on the ward. Was Jack back yet, he wondered?

He stepped out into the farmyard, carefully closing the door behind him to keep in what little warmth remained. The first thing that struck him was how quiet it all was. Yes, of course there was the thud and rumble of the big guns a bare few miles away to his left, but here, just here, the late morning air was still. So still he could hear the slow movements of Madame's milk cow as she wrenched at the few remaining tufts of grass in the meadow and chewed them slowly between her big, yellow teeth. The major turned his head to contemplate her. A good old thing, solid, dependable, and, though she was barely giving any milk any more, the little she did give was crucial to the men.

With something between a smile and a sigh, he shook his shoulders and set off across the yard. If he wasn't tending to the bumf, he'd better go and check on his one remaining patient. A sound chap, that lieutenant, eager to get back to his men. Good lad.

***

Jack kicked at a pile of rusty ironwork. It toppled over with a satisfying jangle and crashed in a heap all over the tiny yard. The skinny, slimy, slippery little runt had told him nothing, nothing, nothing.

He'd seemed scared enough at first, when Jack had laid into him, telling him he knew he was in cahoots with the big Frenchman and demanding that he tell Jack all the details. It hadn't taken long, though, for the beery haze in the man's brain to clear, and for the devious bastard to start denying everything and then to begin to ask just who Jack was that he thought he had the right to know. Once Private bloody Sidney Slater, 1st London (City of London) Regiment (Royal Fusiliers), established that Jack was a civilian, a medical orderly, a nobody, he'd simply shrugged and sauntered off.

"Whatever it is you think you know," he'd said as he left, "you don't know anything. And best for you if you keep it that way, know what I mean?" And he'd gone, leaving Jack exasperated, frustrated, baffled. What now? He'd alerted the private and put him on his guard, and had learned absolutely nothing more about what was actually going on. Hard-bitten journalist, eh? Useless half-wit, more like. He gave the ironmongery another half-hearted kick. Well, he'd better make his way back to the CCS and report to Olivier and the major on his magnificent exploits.

***

It was the sound of the flies that roused the man from his torpor. He had no idea how long he'd been sitting there, but his fingers were sticking together with the boy's drying blood, and the sun was well past midday.

He couldn't look at the child. The smell and the sound of the feasting flies was enough. He bent double, his head between his knees, and retched and retched until there was nothing left in his stomach but bitter bile. He wiped at his mouth with his sleeve, and curled up, hands over his head, beside the dead child, shuddering. He pressed his face into the hard ground to stop himself screaming. He mustn't let them win, he mustn't let them win, he mustn't let them win. He had to be stronger. The children needed him, now more than ever.

Slowly the shuddering stopped. With a huge effort he sat up, then knelt beside the boy's body. Keeping his eyes clenched shut, he drew off his own ragged jacket and laid it as a blanket over the little corpse, drawing it right up to the child's chin. Carefully, he allowed himself to look.

How beautiful he looked, how peaceful. His cheeks so pale, his eyelids almost transparent. He had gone beyond this filthy world, and was utterly pure.

So that's where he'd gone wrong before. He'd tried to keep the boys as boys, still caught up in all this earthly torment. He needed to take that torment on himself and free them to be themselves, to be lovely, carefree, full of light. It would be hard, God knows, but he would steel himself and face it all for their sakes.

***

Auguste was far from happy. The deal with the British private had

121

gone well enough. A few packs of smutty postcards left over from some time before Noah left the ark, and some rancid bottles of Hervé's home-brew mixed with ethanol nicked from the Yanks further up the line. Like taking candy from a baby, as the Americans would say. A delightful expression, made all the more enjoyable by the fact that the Yanks were all babies themselves. And had lots and lots of candy.

But then he'd caught sight of the little private weaving down the street arm in arm with one of the officers from the first aid post out at the Blanchards' place. It didn't look good. He'd have to find out what the hell was going on. He'd followed quietly behind, and waited just out of sight. When the private swaggered round the corner, he gasped with surprise to see Auguste there. He looked terrified. So he should be. Auguste grabbed him by the shoulder and pressed him against the wall, pinning him down with a forearm across the soldier's throat.

"What did you tell him, you little bastard?" he hissed in Sidney's ear. "What did the fucker want?"

Sidney shook his head against the big man's weight and anger. "I didn't tell him nothing. He doesn't know nothing. He's just a fucking civvy who's got a bee in his bonnet."

Sidney's voice began to rise with self-righteousness.

"You better not have spoken," Auguste whispered, leaning harder into Sidney. "A squeak and I'll find you. You know that, don't you?"

He pushed the soldier away.

Sidney nodded vigorously and scuttled thankfully down the narrow alley-way, rubbing his bruised throat.

Auguste went back to waiting. A civilian, eh, not an officer? Well, that made it easier.

He heard the clattering and the swearing coming from the courtyard and smiled. Good. An angry man was a blind man. He leant against the wall with his arms crossed, ready for the moment when the bastard would first catch sight of him.

He didn't have long to wait.

***

Jack's head was filled with self-reproach when he rounded the corner and almost collided with the big Frenchman who was leaning against the wall, arms crossed, looking straight at him. He snapped to a halt, suddenly afraid. He'd brought Sidney to this place because he knew it was isolated and they wouldn't be overheard. Now he was alone with this silent, sombre man. He tried to brazen it out.

"Good afternoon," he said, and went as if to walk on.

Auguste thrust out his arm to block his way.

"Not so fast, young man, not so fast. I hear you've been asking questions about me, and that makes me very unhappy."

Jack squared up to the Frenchman. Perhaps this was his chance.

"And why should that make you unhappy if you didn't have something to hide?" He was aware that his voice sounded thin and a good deal less defiant than his words.

The Frenchman's expression barely changed as he swung his arm round and punched Jack in the side of the head. He felt himself slammed against the wall, and then more blows, to his face, to his chest. He curled on the ground, arms over his head, coughing uncontrollably as blood ran down into his eyes and spilled out of his mouth.

And all the while he could hear the Frenchman speaking, punctuating his sentences with blows.

"Because, you nosy English bastard, my business is my business, and if I want to profit out of this goddam stupid war by selling liquor and tobacco and porn, then it's no fucking business but my own, and I will not," and here he swung a kick at Jack which caught him on the knee. It felt as if his kneecap had shattered, "I will not," another kick, "have anyone getting in my way." There was a pause, and then a mighty kick to Jack's stomach. Every ounce of breath was knocked out of him. He welcomed the blackness which swept down.

***

123

He had no idea how long he'd been unconscious. It seemed as though it might be evening. It was certainly cold, and he thought it might be dark, but as his eyelids seemed to be swollen shut, it was rather hard to tell. His knee was throbbing, his stomach hurt, and his shoulders were aching dreadfully. He tried to shift position. It was only then he realised that he was lying on hard, stony ground, tied hand and foot. He sensed rather than saw that the Frenchman was kneeling beside him. Jack felt himself being pulled this way and that. He tried not to let the man know he was awake. He'd much rather not have another beating. He was puzzled, though, as to what the man was doing. Was he robbing him? Well, good luck with that came the sudden thought. His lips twitched in something that might have been a smile. A penknife, a handful of coins and a filthy handkerchief. What riches! But then he realised that the man wasn't taking things out of his pockets, he was thrusting things into them. Cold, hard, bony things that pressed into his sides and his groin. Then he felt himself being lifted up, and, with a grunt, the man threw him away from him.

Jack waited for the pain of smashing down against the ground, but there was no ground. He fell, and then he hit hard, ice-cold water. And sank.

The man had filled his pockets with stones and thrown him into the canal.

And all for cigarettes and booze.

Jack felt the familiar hot hurt in his chest as his lungs fought to find oxygen.

And the water was so cold.

Stupid, stupid, stupid.

It had all been such a stupid mistake.

CHAPTER 12

Alex was up before first light, his mother still wrapped in her quilted coverlet, her hair loose on the pillow. He paused and looked at her for a moment before tiptoeing past, pulling on his jumper and the trousers stiff with the night's cold. He picked up his boots, and waited until he had slipped out of the barely open door before pushing his feet into them and carefully tying the awkward leather laces. He had heard all sorts of strange groaning clanking noises close by in the night, and he was determined to find out what was going on.

The yard looked eerie in the flat grey light of dawn, familiar shapes bulked into threatening shadows, and the silence, it seemed, absolute. Then Alex heard it, the scrape of a thick-soled boot against the cobbles, the strike and hiss of a match. There was a soldier just round the corner, on the road beside the farmhouse. Alex marched towards the noise, his own boots flinty on the ground. He didn't want to surprise the soldier. He knew these men meant him no harm, but he knew too that they were tired and jumpy. And you didn't surprise a tired man holding a gun.

As he rounded the corner, Alex stopped dead and nearly let out a gasp. There was a huge monster looming behind the soldier, one dead eye staring over the man's shoulder and centred on Alex. The soldier grinned.

'Hello there, youngster, it's a big fucker, isn't it?' Alex didn't understand the words, but he understood the soldier's smile and his gesture of pride, of ownership. The soldier liked the monster, a lot.

The soldier looked around him. There seemed to be no one else in sight. 'Fancy a quick shufti, eh?' He set down his rifle, and lifted up a corner of the heavy netting which had been draped over the huge machine. Metal gleamed black in the shadows. Mud had dried and flaked along its sides, caking the flat plates of its tracks. 'Like a caterpillar, right?' explained the soldier. 'Can go over anything. Shell holes, trenches, barbed wire, the whole ruddy lot.' Reaching forward, he grasped Alex under the arms and swung him round so that he was standing high up on the flank of the machine, one of its guns sticking out beside him, pointing back down the road it must have crept up overnight before being hidden here. Alex crouched down and tried to peer through the gunsights into the black interior of the beast. All he could see was darkness.

***

Murray hadn't slept. Partly the sound of the troops moving, the creaking of the ordnance being dragged into place, the muttered orders had kept him unwillingly alert. More than that, though, he was concerned, baffled, disturbed by Jack's disappearance. Where the hell had he got to? He must have had some kind of accident. Nothing else would have kept him from his duties. Or from the farmer's wife. Murray had eyes on him. He could see what was what. So where had the scrawny bugger got to?

Murray moved himself gingerly to the side of the bed, then swung his legs down until his feet found his slippers. At least with no one else left on the ward now he wouldn't disturb anyone if he went for a bit of a wander. Despite the tight agony in his back, he felt he couldn't stay still a moment longer.

Reaching for the stick which the orderly had found for him, Murray shuffled into his dressing gown and then made his slow way down between the rows of empty beds, their pillows piled up, the mattresses neatly rolled. How much longer would they stand silent and empty, Murray wondered. Not much longer at all, he guessed, judging by the tension and the noises in the night.

Getting to the huge barn doors, he swung open one of the massive gates just enough for him to slip through, closing it gently behind him to keep such warmth as there was trapped on the ward. Perhaps later he'd be able to go back to bed and get some sleep at last.

In the dim light of the dawn, Murray made his way across the farmyard and leaned against the gate into the orchard. The ruins of the village on the far horizon looked particularly stark against the cold grey sky. He shivered, only partly from the cold.

'Couldn't sleep either, eh, old man?' Murray started as the major's voice sounded quietly beside him, and he saw the little doctor standing quietly in the shadows just beyond the gate. He too was gazing over the fields towards the ruined village.

'No, no,' Murray conceded. 'I don't know whether it was the creaking and groaning of the guns coming up, the pain in my back, or worry about Jack, or all of it and more, but no, I couldn't sleep. There are times I wonder whether I'll ever sleep again.'

The major looked thoughtfully at the young soldier. 'You'll be well enough in time, young man, I have no doubt. You've a strong body and a good heart. They'll see you through.'

'Maybe,' replied Murray, almost grudgingly. 'Neither seem much protection against machine guns and shrapnel.'

'No, indeed. No, indeed.' The major fell silent for a moment, sensing that what he had meant as encouragement had seemed facile and obtuse to the wounded lieutenant. For a long while neither spoke, then, 'Well,' said the major. 'What have you done with my orderly, then? Trussed him up and tucked him under your mattress to give yourself a free hand with the lovely Madeleine? If so, I'd like him back please. I have no doubt I'm going to be needing him before too long. Him and many more besides.'

Murray snorted, acknowledging the doctor's attempt to lighten the mood.

'I doubt whether the lovely Madeleine, as you call her, even knows I exist, and as for having Jack tucked away somewhere, my mattress is quite lumpy enough, thank you, without having a tubercular journalist coughing and spluttering away underneath it. In fact, to be honest,' Murray turned so that he was facing the major, 'I am damned worried about Jack. I barely know him, it's true, but he didn't strike me as any kind of a shirker. What do you think's happened to him, sir?'

'Nothing good, I'm afraid. You're right. Jack's a good man and a hard worker. He wouldn't just disappear without a word. He hinted to me yesterday that he'd heard something in the village which might have had something to do with these boys disappearing. He didn't want to say more. Told me it was pure speculation and he needed more proof. I wonder whether Olivier knows anything more. Jack might have confided in him, as he used to be a policeman and understands these things much better than some old army quack. I'll ask him when he gets here, if he does. There's no knowing, these days, about anything.' And the major sank into a melancholy silence, gazing out over the fence, wondering what the bright bitter day would bring.

***

The man stood looking down at the little group where they lay, sheltered by the trees at the edge of the little glade. He sank to his knees and bowed his head, shivering, partly from the cold. He had had to bury his jacket, and all their other clothes, his and Jean-Marie's. It would have been better if he could have burned them, but They might have seen the smoke. They had gone down to the stream together, he and the boy. They had both stripped completely naked, and then he'd washed them both, carefully removing every last smear of blood, even scraping under their fingernails with the very tip of his knife until they were both quite clean, and no sign or scent of blood remained. He couldn't remember much of the rest of that night, nor of the morning that followed.

He knew he had taken a blanket from the pile in the hut, and cut it in two - one half for him, one half for Jean-Marie. He had wrapped

128

the boy carefully, explaining to him where he was now, and how it would be his job to help the others to cross into the pure land where he now lived. A land with no blood.

It was the blood he had to guard against.

***

Madeleine had come running out of the house, calling Alex's name in a shrill, harsh cry quite unlike her usual voice. She had woken from uneasy dreams to find the boy's bed cold and empty, his clothes gone, the child nowhere to be found. The still, chill silence through the house was more than she could bear.

She stood in the farmyard, shouting his name, her shawl tight over her dress, her dress buttoned anyhow, her hair barely pinned and already hanging unsteadily around her face.

Murray and the doctor had turned as one and stepped towards the panicking woman as she lunged, jerking her head backwards and forwards, searching, searching for her son.

'Alex, Alex...'

Then a voice. 'Maman, I'm here.'

Madeleine and the doctor hurtled round the corner of the farmhouse to see the boy standing proudly on the huge machine, a soldier awkwardly holding the camouflage netting in one hand while trying to reach for his rifle with the other. As Murray made his slow way to where the others were standing, it seemed sudden utter mayhem. Madeleine had pulled the boy to her and was holding him tight against her chest while shouting at the soldier, at the child, tears coursing down her cheeks, her hair tumbling in a black tide across her shoulders. The sentry was standing stiffly to attention, being harangued simultaneously by his irate corporal, an emphatically upset major and an almost hysterically distraught mother. If things hadn't been so worrying, it would have been farcical.

Murray limped carefully over to Madeleine and touched her arm lightly to get her attention. 'Madame, is the child alright? L'enfant, bon?'

Madeleine swung round to face him and graced him with a brilliant, radiant smile. 'Oui, oui, tout bon.' She spoke rapidly, dividing her attention between Murray and her son, by turns berating the child and caressing him, telling Murray the tale of her fright at finding the boy gone, her delight at seeing him safe. Murray couldn't understand the words, but heard the change as the panic gradually subsided, and the fear and anger modulated to a gentle, teasing chiding.

Gradually the group broke up, the sentry replaced while the corporal led the careless culprit away. He would probably be put on a charge. Whether that was something to be sorry or glad about he really didn't know. A week in the brig, or being in the Show? And all for being nice to a lonely boy. It was a fucking confusing world, that was for sure. Stuff it, and stuff the lot of them.

**

When Olivier arrived at the farm half an hour later, the excitement had completely died down. The major was in his little office, going through orders and requisitions, initialling and signing and sighing. Everything in duplicate or triplicate, everyone covering their own backs. He flung his pen down in disgust as Olivier put his head round the door.

'Is that a sign you need some coffee, dear major?' asked Olivier.

'Ah, coffee, yes, coffee. If it wasn't for that damned moustache and the fact that you stink of tobacco, I'd say you were an angel, old man.'

'Indeed, if I'm an angel, the Almighty must be desperately short-staffed. Coffee it is. Shall I call you when it's made and we can drink in front of the fire?'

'Capital, yes, thank you,' and the major picked up his pen and resumed signing with renewed vigour.

The coffee, or what passed for coffee (mostly dandelion leaves and chicory, Olivier guessed) had been drunk, and now the two men sat, their boots stretched towards the small fire, each with their pipes in their hands.

'So, old man,' began the major. 'Any idea what's happened to my orderly? I don't suppose he said anything to you before he went up to the village? Any clue as where he might have gone?'

'Well, yes and no,' Olivier replied cautiously. 'He did speak to me, but as to where he was going or what he intended to do, no, I've no idea.'

'But he did speak to you?' the little major probed gently.

'Yes, he asked my opinion about a conversation he had overheard. He wanted to know what I made of it. To be honest, I wasn't sure what to make of it, and that's what I told him. It was just bits and pieces of sentences he'd caught, something about payments and deliveries, between a bit of a dodgy British soldier Jack had run across earlier and some local Jack'd never seen before. From his description, I have an idea who it might have been. One of my more unsavoury compatriots, a chancer. Probably a black-marketeer, I'd say, but I've no proof, and neither did Jack. What these men were talking about, whether it had anything to do with these boys going missing, there was simply no way of knowing.'

'D'you think the young fool might have gone looking for more proof?' asked the major, pulling on his pipe.

'Yes, yes I do.' Olivier paused, thinking through what might have happened and what he might now need to do. 'I believe he probably went after the British soldier, I think he said he was called Sidney something, but I'm afraid I don't really recall, or else he might have tried to find out more about our local thug and all round bad boy, the profoundly inappropriately named Auguste Bonnefoy. And that would be my fault, because I told Jack that's who it probably was he'd seen talking to the soldier. The description fitted, and Auguste is exactly the kind of bastard to be up to his elbows in any kind of vice so long as there was money to be made. He's not a bugger to be taken lightly, though. He hasn't survived this long without being able to take care of himself. I better get down to the village and see what's what, and whether the cops have picked up a whisper of anything going on.'

With that, the ex-policeman stood up decisively, knocked his pipe against the chimney-piece to clear it of any last embers, tucked it into his pocket and strode out of the door. The major shook his head and took one last pull at his own pipe before getting more slowly to his feet and going back to his paperwork. 'A rum business,' he muttered as he settled back at his desk, seeming to include everything around him in that uneasy condemnation.

**

The man put the hoe back in the corner of the lean-to and gazed over to where the children lay. They were each so special and so precious, and they all cared for each other so gently. Their latest friend, Philippe, had brought one of his books with him. The man had been careful to tuck it in beside him, inside the piece of cloth he had wrapped him in once he had drained him of his blood and washed him clean. He was sure the others would be glad of Philippe's skill with reading, his love of story-telling. He could keep them entertained for hours as they lay and listened to him.

That'd be more than Philippe's mother had ever done, or the curly-haired tubby little toddler she doted on, a child so dark, so different, so noisy and energetic where the seven-year old Philippe was so pale and quiet that it was sure that they had never shared the same father. It seemed just as sure, too, that all the mother's care went to the cuckoo in the nest. Well, no more. Philippe was safe here with his friends. They would all care for each other here.

He lit his pipe, and leaned back against a tree, looking fondly at the five small mounds. Well begun, half done, he could remember his grandmother saying. Yes, half done. A good job, well begun. And he sat silent, alert for the giggling of the boys as they played together, just below the level of his hearing.

***

Olivier strode purposefully into the little gendarmerie, only to be brought to a full stop by the outstretched arm of the desk sergeant. 'Excuse me, sir, may I ask your business? You can't just go marching in here as if you own the place, you know.'

'I apologise. My name is Olivier Verger, retired Commandant of police. I need to see your superior officer urgently.'

'My superior officer, monsieur Verger,' the sergeant lightly emphasising the civilian title, 'is not in the office, and will not be returning until tomorrow afternoon at the earliest, having been called to headquarters on confidential official business. That makes the superior officer here,' he paused for effect, 'me. So just what can I do for you, monsieur Verger? What is it that seems to you so very urgent?'

Chapter 13

Olivier's conversation with the gendarmerie had not been disastrous, but it had not produced any real results either. His initial flare of anger and impatience at the desk sergeant's patronising self-importance had quickly been replaced by a slightly embarrassed humility as he glimpsed what he must look like from the young man's point of view - an elderly civilian throwing his weight around and shouting the odds for no apparent reason. Cat caught up a tree, probably, or granny lost her knitting wool. Didn't he know there was a war on? Olivier had taken a deep breath and literally stepped back, so as to look less of a lunatic to the gendarme.

'I do apologise, you're right, I have been extremely rude. Please, may I start again?'

The young man nodded warily.

'It is true that I used to be a Commandant with the Sûreté, down in Lyons. But perhaps more important now is that I come from here, and came back to live here just over two years ago to take care of my elderly mother. Perhaps you knew her, Mme Eleanore Verger? The pink house just past the baker's?'

Another careful nod.

'Be that as it may, the fact is that for the last few months I have been helping out around the village wherever I can - there aren't that many able-bodied men around not already in uniform and doing their bit.' Olivier made a slight gesture towards the stiff young man. 'Even an old codger like me can be a help cutting wood or carrying stuff, eh?'

Another nod. Almost, perhaps, a smile.

'The thing is, I've been helping out at Mme Blanchard's farm up the road, you know, where the Brits have got their first aid post?'

'I know it,' acknowledged the gendarme carefully.

'And something's come to my notice, well, two things really. Both of which you probably know about, but, well, I thought I'd ask you if you had any news.'

Olivier paused, not quite sure how to proceed. A few boys playing hooky and a medical orderly going AWOL. It was difficult to explain quite why he felt so alarmed, why he was sure that something disastrous had happened to Jack, and why he knew in his heart of hearts that the little boys weren't just being mischievous.

'And these two things would be?' prompted the desk sergeant, reaching for his pen and holding it poised over the inkwell, ready to make an official note of what Olivier had to say.

The ex-policeman gathered his thoughts.

'The first is fairly recent. A medical orderly from the Casualty Clearing Station has gone missing. He set off saying he was coming up to the village yesterday morning and hasn't been seen since.'

The gendarme laid his pen down and looked about to speak.

'Before you say anything, sergeant, let me just add a couple of relevant details.' Olivier's tone caught the gendarme's attention. He picked up his pen again. 'Jack Cadogan, the orderly,' Olivier went on, 'is a very conscientious young man, dedicated to his work. He would not just disappear like this, especially when, especially when - '

'Especially when we seem to be about to see something none of us should talk about?'

'Thank you, sergeant, perfectly expressed. Jack would not just disappear when we seem to be on the edge of something none us of should mention.'

'But he is a grown man, a civilian, an Englishman - what do you expect us to be able to do, Commandant?'

'Little, I know, perhaps nothing, except to keep your eyes open in case he turns up, perhaps injured or ill, you know?'

Olivier watched as the sergeant of gendarmerie noted down in his careful copperplate the details of Jack's name, his occupation, the date when he went missing.

'You said, Commandant, that there were two things?'

'Yes, and they may be related, or perhaps maybe not. The thing is, a few of us up at the farm have heard about the boys who have been going missing round about - '

The desk sergeant laid down his pen and folded his arms across his chest.

'And what exactly is it that you have heard?'

'Very little, sergeant, very little. Mme Blanchard has a friend whose little son has not been seen in very nearly two weeks - '

'That'll be Mme Mardel's boy,' interrupted the sergeant.

'Yes, yes, indeed, Paul I believe he's called. Because of Mme Blanchard, I became slightly involved in seeing if I could help find out what had become of the boy, and then one conversation led to another, and it seems that three or four other little lads are missing from roundabout.'

'That may or may not be the case,' answered the sergeant with a frown. 'But what on earth has any of this got to do with you, let alone with a missing British orderly?'

Olivier had smiled ruefully.

'A very good question, sergeant, and one I can only answer with suspicions and suppositions. The thing is,' here Olivier leant forward on the high desk separating the reception area from the rest of the gendarmerie, 'the thing is, because of Mme Blanchard, and her friend, and Mme Blanchard's own son, little Alex - ' The sergeant nodded to show he knew about the boy. 'Because of them, and because there's been a bit of a lull in the proceedings over there,' nodding towards the distant German lines, 'just now, the few of us up at the farm got to talking, wondering just what might be going on with these boys, and then Jack, the orderly, he overheard something in the village which seemed as though it might have had something to do with it -'

'Overheard what, exactly?'

Olivier summoned his thoughts. He wanted to give as clear and helpful account as he could.

'Jack Cadogan heard snatches of a conversation between a British private and Auguste Bonnefoy - '

'Bonnefoy, eh? There's a man drags a stink wherever he goes.'

'Yes.' Olivier paused and then went on. 'It seemed as if Bonnefoy and this British private were doing some business together, they were talking about deliveries, and goods and payment. But it was all very vague, and I am afraid when Cadogan told me about it and asked my opinion, I told him it was all hearsay and innuendo, and that he had no hard evidence that they were up to anything, let alone that they were up to anything with the missing children.'

The desk sergeant looked sympathetically at the older man.

'So you're worried that this Cadogan man may have gone after Bonnefoy to try and find out more, and that Bonnefoy might not have taken too kindly to him sticking his nose into whatever mischief he's up to?'

'That, sergeant, is it, precisely, in a nutshell. I know Auguste of old, and he's a nasty piece of work. Jack's a skinny individual, TB, I think, no meat on him, but he fancies himself a bit of a roving reporter, he was out in South Africa, you know, and he's got a bee in his bonnet about rescuing these missing children, and, well - '

Olivier had dropped his hands in a gesture of baffled helplessness. It was true, there was hardly anything to go on, and even less the gendarmes could do. But the sergeant had taken pity on him, and had agreed to keep an eye out for Jack, and to let Olivier know if he had any news.

As for the children, well, that was a different matter, and really he had no idea what, if anything, was going on there. Different jurisdictions, you see, and then, of course, the war...

Olivier had nodded and thanked the sergeant for his time and for his thoughtfulness, and then made his way rather despondently back to the farm.

**

The man had watched big Claude Bastide the longest. Was he too old to fit in, perhaps? At ten he was much older than almost all the others in years, but he was young in mind - a hulking, gentle, guileless child. The other village children sometimes mocked him, sometimes helped him, but usually they just left him alone. He lived with his aunt – the mother, he'd been told, was working as a nurse. The aunt was baffled, not unkind, but unclear how to handle this child who had a young man's body and a baby's mind.

The man waited and observed and noted, unsure whether he would be right, whether it would be right. In the end he decided that the boy's size made him an easy prey for those who would harm him. He too needed protection. He reached down for his knife.

**

Night had fallen. There'd been no more news.

Olivier looked at them all as they sat together round the kitchen table. They were a heterogeneous group brought together by strange chance and urgent commitment. Madeleine sat a little way apart from the rest of them, her hands folding and refolding one of Alex's little jumpers.

Murray sat at the head of the table. He was the only one of them who seemed to have a sense of energy and direction. His back was still held in a stiff swathe of bandages which gave him a misleadingly military bearing. Only his pallor and the twitching of the fingers holding the pencil betrayed a little of what he had been through, a little of the tension he was feeling now.

The major sat to Murray's right, his chair at an angle to the table, as though he were only half part of the group.

Beyond him, Olivier sat, solid and still, his rough, cracked hands resting on the table.

The major cleared his throat.

'I think we need to get some sense of order into the proceedings.'

They all raised their eyes to him.

'Madame,' he addressed Madeleine in her own language, with careful, school-learned courtesy. 'Might we have some coffee, if there is enough?'

Madeleine rose, laying the little jumper carefully on her chair, as gently as if it were her son. She walked across the room and filled a saucepan from the pump at the sink. All the men sat and watched her graceful, accustomed movements as she set the water on the range, fetched the carefully-hoarded coffee from the little box on the shelf above, and measured out generous spoonfuls of the powder into the big old enamel jug. They were all still as the water gradually simmered then boiled, and Madeleine took a cloth to hold the saucepan and pour the boiling water onto the coffee grounds.

The rare, rich smell of real coffee filled the room.

Madeleine reached down four bowls from the shelf above the sink and placed one in front of each place, then she went round and filled the bowls with the dark, steaming liquid. Finally, she placed a brimming jug of fresh milk in the centre of the table, and sat down again, lifting the jumper and lying it carefully across her knee.

Each of the men reached out and took his coffee. Murray and the major poured a little milk into theirs. Olivier cradled his bowl full of strong black coffee, holding the steam to his face and sniffing in the heady scent. Still not a word had been spoken.

'Thank you,' said the major to Madeleine. 'Now then,' he turned to Murray. 'I believe you've been making a map.'

Murray nodded and spread out the piece of paper which lay in front of him so that everyone at the table could see it. Madeleine stood and reached down a candlestick. She lit the remains of the candle wedged in it, and put it in the centre of the table so that the light was cast over the pencil markings which Murray had made on the paper.

'It seems to have started here.' He pointed to an area near the centre of the paper. 'Although of course we can't be sure. These are only the ones we've heard about. The ones that have been spoken of.'

Madeleine gazed intently at the rough map, as though just looking at the pattern of small crosses with their names and dates could reveal some meaning, some purpose, some way of making it stop. Her hands gripped the table tightly, but she didn't speak.

The major pushed the paper towards Olivier.

'Monsieur, do you have any thoughts? You know the area and the people better than any of us, apart of course, from Madame.'

Olivier nodded and drew the paper towards him. He rested his eyes on the marks that Murray had made. He touched each one with his finger.

'Madame,' he said, raising his eyes to Madeleine. 'Do you have more paper?'

Madeleine rose and went across to the linen chest in the corner of the room. She took out a sheet of brown paper from a shop. It had been used and then carefully folded, stored against future need. She took it across to the table and laid it in front of the ex-policeman. Olivier took the pencil from Murray's fingers and started to write carefully in one corner of the brown paper.

Paul Mardel, 6

François Ladurie, 14

Michel Dubois, 5

Jean-Marie Leclerc, 4

Philippe Castaing, 7

'What do we know about these children? What do we notice?' Olivier asked the others, resting his eyes on each in turn.

'Apart from the Ladurie lad they are all very young. Not babies, but all still children.' This from Murray.

'Hmm,' Olivier looked thoughtfully at the paper and made a note underneath the list. 'The youngest is 4, the oldest 14. I think we need to come back to that in a minute. What else? However obvious, however strange.'

'They are all boys,' Madeleine spoke for the first time since they'd all been gathered together. 'They are small boys.' And she lifted Alex's jumper, holding it against her heart.

A silence fell, then Madeleine spoke again. 'There may be one more.'

The men all looked round at her.

'It seems that young Claude Bastide, you know, that big idiot boy from by the canal,' she looked questioningly at Olivier, who nodded his reassurance. 'It seems he didn't go home this evening when it grew dark. His aunt sent word for everyone to look out for him.'

'And just how old is he, Madame?' asked Olivier gently.

'Ten, I believe, yes, ten. He was born just after there was all that fuss about the curé's young nephew. You remember, Olivier, don't you?'

'I remember what you call the fuss. My mother wrote to me about it in quite some detail. I was down in Lyons at the time, but yes, I think you're right, that must have been ten years ago.'

Murray broke in.

'Did I understand Madame correctly? Did she say this latest boy, this Claude, is ten years old? That makes him nearly the oldest to have disappeared so far, doesn't it? There's quite a spread in age, now, isn't there? Do you think that is significant, monsieur?' addressing himself to Olivier.

Chapter 14

The early morning was grey and chill. Olivier had sat for a while with Madeleine after the others had left, and discussed with her in quiet tones what he felt he needed to do. She agreed. The chores around the farm could wait awhile. She would do what she could, he would come when he was able. The main thing was to find the boys, and to find Jack.

So it was that now, before the sun had even risen, Olivier had woken in the silent house that had once been his childhood home, and stepped into the cold air. He still felt his mother's presence everywhere. She'd only been dead, what, five months, and there were small remembrances of her scattered throughout the house. Some mending she had started and had then laid aside, meaning to finish when she felt stronger. A candle which still stood by her bedside, next to her prayer book, the candle half burned down, the prayer book still marked at the place she had last looked to for the comfort of God's word.

Olivier himself was not sure what comfort there had been. He knew that he himself had found none. But his mother, a child of a different time, perhaps.

It was an arrangement he had no wish to disturb.

He stood in the street for a while, watching the sky lightening, feeling the thud and shudder of the shells further down the line, hearing the sounds of the village waking up around him.

He'd go down to the café for a bite to eat and see if Marianne had any gossip to tell him about everything that had been happening these last few days. She might, at least, have some idea about what had happened to Jack.

***

It felt different now.

Gabriel Leclerc. Just six years old.

Jean-Marie's older cousin, and a bright, brash, blond boy with a hasty, harsh manner on the surface. He mimicked the behaviour of his brothers – all older, all down the mines – but the man saw that when he was alone he had a different nature.

The boy would take himself across the fields to walk beside the canal, and then sit or lie on his belly, watching the water. He was a hidden dreamer. He needed safeguarding.

The man looked round the little clearing in the wood. This would probably be a good place, he thought, selecting an area as far as possible from where the children lay - best not to disturb them when they're being so quiet. He laid out the stiff tarpaulin he had bought from one of the English soldiers - four eggs and a brace of ragged-looking pigeons it had cost him. Well worth it, though, now that he fully understood what was needed.

He carried over the two fence posts he had brought from home, and hammered them into the hard ground, one at either end of the tarpaulin. He moved slowly and methodically, making sure the posts were solidly set in the soil, and that they stood level, one to the other. He tied the tarpaulin between them, mooring it each end with rope, so that it hung down like a sailor's hammock. He leant his weight down on the makeshift sling. Not strong enough to bear him, but, yes, fine for a boy. Gabriel could rest here while he was being transformed, transmuted, transported. He didn't know what to call the process. While he was being changed.

***

Murray was triumphant. He had decided that morning that, come

144

what may, he was going to stop behaving like a bloody invalid and start getting back in shape. It was obvious that there was some sort of Show going to happen in the next few days or weeks, and he wanted to get back to his men to be with them when the balloon went up. The first step, of course, was to get dressed. He didn't think he'd do much to terrify the Hun charging at them in his pyjamas and dressing-gown. Might shock Boy Jones, though. Murray caught himself chuckling at the thought.

The idea of getting dressed was one thing. Finding his clothes and putting them on was quite a different kettle of fish. First of all there was the finding clothes difficulty. Sitting on his bed and looking up and down the empty ward, Murray realised he had no idea where anything was, nor, now that Jack seemed to have disappeared, no-one he could easily ask. His own clothes, he suddenly realised, had been shredded when he was wounded. And what hadn't been wrecked by the shrapnel had been cut off by the medics. Well, there must be some sort of uniform for him somewhere. He'd just have to go and scavenge for it. Grabbing his walking stick, and thrusting his feet into his slippers, he set off to see who or what he could find to get himself kitted out.

He'd got as far as the sluice room when the major found him.

'So what are you up to in here, young fella?' the little doctor asked, addressing Murray rather more abruptly than usual. He didn't like anybody near his drug cupboard who wasn't supposed to be there.

Murray started.

'Ah, sir, sorry sir. I was just wondering whether I might find some clothes to wear. Something,' Murray looked down diffidently at the washed-thin cotton of the hospital dressing-gown and pyjamas, 'something a bit more soldierly.'

Immediately the major was abashed at his peremptory manner.

'Of course, my boy, of course. A uniform, eh? Only got hospital blues here, I'm afraid. I'll send back up to base for a lieutenant's kit for you, alright? Might take a day or two, and won't be like your smart

145

tailor-made affair, but something that'll do for now, eh?'

Murray felt himself being firmly ushered away from the sluice room and towards his chair in the corner of the courtyard.

He sat down, wrapping the dressing-gown more tightly around him against the cold. He was bemused by the thought that his old uniform had looked like a tailor-made affair. Miranda's attempts at taking up his trousers and taking in his jacket could hardly, by any stretch of the imagination, be called tailoring. He realised with a start that he hadn't written to Miranda since he'd been wounded. When Jack came back, he must ask him for a pencil and some paper.

***

Sylvie was bored. She had finished scrubbing the front step and rubbing it with whitening. She had helped Maman hang out the sheets and clothes on the bushes that ran along behind the cottage. She had swept the floors and put away the pots and pans from the midday meal. And now there was nothing to do. She'd wanted to go with Maman to visit Mme Villefranche and play with her new baby, but Maman had said no, Mme Villefranche was too tired. She had not, said Maman quietly, had an easy time of it. So Maman had gone, and Sylvie was left with nothing to do until she came home again. She tried reading the book the curé had given her, but the letters were small and the book didn't have any pictures. She thought she'd go down to the canal and see if she could catch a frog. She could bring it home with her and he could be her friend and play with her. She wouldn't kiss it though. Absolutely not. Never. No matter what Adèle said about frogs turning into princes if you kissed them. Ugh.

She pulled on her boots, and laced them up as well as she was able, and wrapped a shawl around her shoulders. It was beginning to get really cold.

As she leant over the canal and looked into the dark water, searching for the small dim shapes of frogs, she saw a face looking back up at her.

***

In the clearing, there was no sound but the scuttling of insects and the rustling of small creatures in the dead leaves. Ants hurried to the spot where blood dripped down through the hammock to pool on the cold earth beneath the pale body with the gaping wound across its throat.

CHAPTER 15

16th November, morning onwards

Olivier marched grim-faced into the farmhouse and rapped on the doctor's office door.

'Come,' said the major.

Olivier went in and carefully shut the door behind him. He stood silent for a moment and then,

'They've found him, I'm afraid. Jack, he's been found.'

Olivier saw the little doctor's face close down. The flare of emotion that had been there for tenths of a second was carefully quelled, and his expression became rigorously professional.

He concentrated on screwing the top back onto his fountain pen, laying the pen down on the papers he was attending to, and only then did he look up and meet Olivier's gaze.

'Where? And how is he? I judge from how you entered it is not good news.'

Olivier lowered himself into one of the wooden chairs that stood opposite the doctor's desk.

'No, not good news, not good news at all.' He spoke gently. He realised that he too had fallen back on old habits, and was using the professional voice which had countless times carried ill tidings to anxious relatives. 'He's been found in the canal. The police are bringing his body out now. I thought you should know as soon as possible.'

'Thank you,' said the major. 'That was kind. What will they - what will become of him now?'

'They are taking him to the undertaker's in the village. There'll need to be a post mortem. Doctor Julien will conduct it this afternoon, with Monsieur Philibert, the undertaker, as his assistant. The police would rather not have any delays, particularly in view of what's coming.' Olivier paused. 'Would you like to - would you like me to ask if you could observe?'

The doctor's eyes flared for a moment as he gazed directly at the ex-policeman, then the shutters came down again.

'No, I would not like to observe, not in the least, but I should, I know, it's the least I can do for the lad. So, yes, please, if it were possible for me to be there, could you arrange it?

Olivier nodded, stood and left the room, treading quietly so as not to disturb the doctor in his thoughts.

***

A mummy's boy, this one. Jean-Baptiste Coligny, a few weeks short of five years old. Fluffy blond hair like a duckling, and bright blue eyes. Still sucked his thumb, and had a square of old blanket, limp and grey, which he carried everywhere with him.

The mother had been recently widowed, and dragged herself around the place all day, clutching a damp handkerchief. Everything seemed too much for her, especially the child, whom she intermittently petted and thrust from her, with a harsh injunction to 'Go and play!'

The child would kick about in the narrow street outside the house, and then sit on the front step, waiting until his mother would sweep him up in her arms again and hold him, sobbing, to her black-clad chest.

How could the boy find a path with such a mother? How could he resist the force of the world without the support of friends? The man was determined the boy would be safe from harm from now on.

He stood patiently, shielded from view across from Jean-Baptiste's house. It didn't matter how long he waited. Everything was prepared and ready, and the child would come to him in the end.

***

Walking back from the village in the wake of the post mortem, conducted with care, if not great skill, by the village doctor, both Major Carter and Olivier trod slowly, in a silence full of thoughts unspoken. Sometimes one of them would shake his head, sometimes one of them would grunt in wordless sorrow at what they'd seen. Neither felt able to speak of the grey-skinned corpse, with its odd pink lips and slightly protruding tongue, of the ribs sticking out along the torso, and the blurred and sightless eyes. Jack's skull had been cracked by at least one vicious blow, and perimortem bruising clouded his arms, his stomach and his back. It was not a natural death, nor a gentle one. Someone had hogtied Jack and beaten him and thrown him into the cold canal, weighting him down with stones.

The major snorted, almost as though amused. Olivier turned his head inquiringly.

'It's just that the poor bugger's clothes were worn so thin that the stones simply tore his pockets open. If he'd been better off and better dressed, we might never have found him.'

Olivier nodded in agreement at the doctor's sardonic observation. Jack's Spartan tastes had at least allowed his friends to learn his fate.

The two men paused when they reached the turning into the farmyard.

'Well,' said Olivier, 'I must go and break the news to Madeleine.'

'And I,' concurred the doctor, 'must tell the young lieutenant. And they'd been getting along so well. Oh hell and damnation!' He kicked at a stone with such violence that it flew from one side of the yard to the other, then he stood still, and, with a deep breath, brought his emotions back under control. He stepped out briskly towards the CCS, calling out, 'Coverdale, Lieutenant Coverdale, could I have a word, young man?'

Meanwhile Olivier turned towards the farmhouse and pushed open the heavy wooden door.

**

It was nearly dusk when little Jean-Baptiste came staggering out into the street, pushed from the house by his sobbing mother.

'Go, just go and be outside for a while, I can't stand any more of your noise,' and she slammed the door.

Jean-Baptiste simply stood in the gutter, his face smeared with tears and snot.

The man walked towards him and spoke gently.

**

Madeleine sat at the table, her hands still in her lap. She knew that Olivier did not bring good news, from the way he had come into the house and said he had something to tell her. Was it the children? Had little Paul been found? Was he -?

Olivier halted her racing thoughts.

'It's Jack, I'm afraid, that orderly from the CCS with the perfect Parisian French. He's been found dead, murdered.'

Madeleine looked Olivier in the eye.

'Murdered? Murdered? Is there not enough death around here already? Why should that polite young man have been murdered? What for? And who? Who's done such a vile thing?'

'I fear it's something to do with the missing children,' Olivier replied in a leaden voice. 'The fellow had asked my advice about how to find out more about what was going on, and I suggested he go down to the village and root around a bit, watching and listening at the café, you know the sort of thing.'

Madeleine nodded.

'I fear I sent him to his death,' Olivier went on.

Madeleine reached out and laid her hand on his. She had no words to comfort him, nor any way to express the dismay which gripped her.

The boys disappearing. Jack killed. And always the guns, the relentless, monstrous, thundering guns.

It was too much.

***

Across the yard, Murray and the major were also sitting in silence, Murray leaning against the wall at the head of his narrow bed, the doctor sitting at its foot.

'The idiot, the blithering, stupid, well-meaning, gormless idiot.' Murray cried out, banging his head back against the wall in pure frustration. 'A sick man, a medic, a stand-up, decent fellow with not a bad bone in his body. It's awful enough out there,' Murray gestured sketchily towards the front line, 'where it's all such a bloody mess. But at least they're soldiers. At least they're giving the Hun what for. But Jack! Murdered! In a tiny French village in the back end of nowhere, and for what? It's not right, sir, it's just not bally right!'

'No, it's not, lieutenant. It's far from right,' replied the doctor somberly. 'But in his way Jack was a soldier too, a soldier in the army of the good. D'you know he'd got kicked off the foreign correspondent column in his paper for being too mouthy about what went on in Africa with the Boers, and the camps and their insufferable women?'

Murray shook his head. He hadn't known.

'That's what he told me. If I had to guess, I'd say he was quite proud of having kicked up a fuss. That's why he was sent off to Paris to write about painting. That's where he learnt his French.'

The major reached for the pipe in his pocket, and, sticking it in his mouth, unlit, he drew on the stem.

'Always on the side of the underdog, our Jack. Ah well.' The little doctor stood and shook his head. 'Well, I'd best be off and write to his next of kin. A father, I believe, and a sister, I think, if remember rightly.'

He left, and Murray stayed, leaning against the bedhead, thoughts of Jack, and death, and violence, and distant, unreachable sisters filling his mind.

***

'No, no, I don't want to. No, that can't be right. No, please, not that.'

The man was pacing round and round the little glade, shaking, muttering, yelling. The boy sat, saying nothing. The man had held his hand as they walked towards the woods, and now the boy was sitting on the bare earth, his back against a tree. He watched the man warily. He was used to his mother shouting and wailing, but this seemed different. This big man was trembling. His face was wet with tears. And he seemed to be talking to someone the little boy could not see.

Suddenly the man stopped dead and drew himself up, squaring his shoulders.

'Very well then,' he muttered, much more quietly than before. 'You don't need to go on any more. If that's what must be, then yes, of course, I will do my best.'

His voice shook, and the tears still flowed.

He walked over to where the tousled-haired child was sitting gazing at him with wide eyes.

'Come, lad, you'd like a lie-down now, wouldn't you?' And lifting him in one swift movement he carried him over and laid him on the makeshift, brown-stained hammock.

The boy watched wordless as the man reached down to his belt and drew out a big hunting knife.

'It's for the best, lad, you'll be safe now, with your friends, in the

Pure Land,' and he swept the knife across the child's throat.

As the blood pulsed and flowed, the man knelt down beside the dying child, bowed his head, placed his lips to the wound and drank his blood.

CHAPTER 16

17ᵗʰ November, dawn onwards

Olivier knew in his bones that Auguste Bonnefoy had something to do with Jack's murder, even if he may not have been the one to beat him, hit him over the head and throw him, tied and weighted down, into the canal. Though he wouldn't put it past him. Far from it. He was a nasty piece of work, a beastly, bulging bully. Always had been, always would be. And quite capable of cold-blooded murder if his own interests were threatened.

But short of taking his bones out and laying them on the police-station counter, Olivier didn't know how he was going to convince the police that Bonnefoy was involved.

He'd have to find a way to get at the truth.

Bonnefoy would be a hard nut to crack. The English soldier Jack had spoken of, perhaps not so much.

The sky was barely beginning to lighten when Olivier left home, and made his way to the baker's, hard by the café. A roll, almost too hot to hold, fresh from the oven, and perhaps a word or two with the baker. Working all night, snatching moments here and there away from the heat of the bakery, Emmanuel sometimes saw things that passed the rest of the village by.

'So, Manou, how goes it?' Olivier asked the white-haired, white-skinned man, bleached with flour dust and a lifetime's lack of sunlight.

'It goes, Olivier, it goes. Sometimes it's better than others. I have a feeling it's going to be one of the less good times soon enough,' and he gestured with his head towards the dark shapes of the soldiers' tents stretched out on the edge of the village. 'I guess they're not just here for a change of scenery, eh?'

'Likely not,' Olivier agreed. He paused. 'You heard about the English medic fished out of the canal?'

Manou nodded and turned to face Olivier directly.

'A bad business. Beaten up, chucked in and left to drown, I heard.'

Olivier gave a half smile.

'Not much you don't hear, is there?'

Manou shrugged.

'Hear anything at all about what was behind it?'

'So you're not just here to savour the quality of my baking?' Manou smiled in turn.

'Your baking is a delight every day of the year, as well you know, my dear man. Today though, in particular, I want to know whether you've picked up anything about this murder? I'm after the bastard who killed the Englishman. This Jack, he seemed to me a good man, fundamentally on the side of the angels.'

'Hmm,' Manou grunted. 'Yup, I'd heard good things about him. The apothecary was particularly taken with him. Said he was a quiet, respectful, educated man.'

'And so he was,' replied Olivier. 'But I'm not here to give him a testimonial, I'm here to do my damnedest to catch his killer. So, old friend, what do you know?'

'Nothing concrete, nothing you could take to the cops, but everyone - that's to say all the good ladies and those old codgers who can still string two words together - everyone is certain sure that Bonnefoy's behind it. He's got a lot of fingers in a lot of dodgy pies roundabout. It looks as though your Brit was sniffing around one of Bonnefoy's shady schemes, got a bit close, and bang, splash.' The baker

156

gestured as if hitting someone over the head and throwing them over his shoulder.

'That,' growled Olivier, 'is what I was afraid of. And the chance of making Bonnefoy squeal is about the same as the chance of me developing wings and a halo.'

'Not in this life,' Manou agreed, 'and perhaps not even in the life to come. I remember what you got up to back in the day.'

'Hmm, well, you weren't exactly as pure as the driven snow either, as I recall.'

The two men looked at each and smiled, locked in a moment's warmth.

'What about an English soldier hanging around? Anybody seen Bonnefoy with a chap like that?'

'Oh yes, weedy looking little chap, shifty maybe, though hardly in Bonnefoy's league. Been seen in the café with him at least a couple of times, though.'

'I don't suppose you have any idea of his name, or rank, or regiment?' Olivier knew he was clutching at straws.

'I don't, but Jean-Marc will.'

'Jean-Marc the sexton? How on earth would he know anything about English soldiers?'

'Oh, it's not just the English, it's every kind of soldier that's come through here. He decided from early on in the war that it was his responsibility to keep a record of everything that happened here while the war was on. He sees himself as a kind of guardian of the village's memory. Everything that's happened, everyone who's gone to fight, everyone who's been wounded or killed, or who's missing, like your poor Madeleine's man, he notes them down daily in his diary. And all the troops coming through, their nationality, regiment, where they've come from, and, as far as he can, where they're off to. He's got it all. If anyone knows who your little English soldier might be, it'll be Jean-Marc.'

'Well I'll be damned!' Olivier was astonished.

'We've already agreed that's more than likely,' smiled Manou, clapping him on the shoulder. 'I must get back to the ovens, and you, if I'm not mistaken, must be off to talk to Jean-Marc. You know where to find him?'

'Yes, yes indeed. Many thanks, my friend, this is more than I had hoped for,' and Olivier set off striding up the high street and towards the church.

***

Jean-Marc had had no doubt which regiment the English soldier would belong to.

'It'll be the Royal Fusiliers,' he'd said, reaching for the big black accounts books in which he was keeping his records. 'Here we are,' he ran his finger down the spindly writing and stopped triumphantly. 'The Post Office Rifles, this bunch is called. See, I've made a sketch of their cap badge with its funny, pointy cross. They came up just over a week ago, and are camped here until whenever they all have a go at pushing the Boches back again. And yes, I've seen one of their privates hanging around on his own, sitting outside the café nursing a beer. I may have seen him talking to Bonnefoy. Wouldn't swear to it, though. As for a name, well, not the first idea, I'm afraid, chief.'

Jean-Marc slammed the book shut and put it back on the shelf.

'Thank you so much,' said Olivier. 'That's amazing.'

'Glad I could help. But now, if you'll excuse me, I've three graves to dig. Old Louis finally let go last night, and then there's those two Lamarque boys who were shipped back yesterday. Joined up together, fought together, died together - and now who's to look after their old mother and their little sister?'

Jean-Marc opened the door for Olivier, and followed him out into the November morning.

'It's a bad business, a bad business all round, I say,' muttered Jean-Marc, heading for the shed where he kept his tools.

'That it is indeed,' agreed Olivier, turning back towards the village centre and the gendarmerie. It was time to have another word with the sergeant, or with his boss, if he was back yet.

***

It was the sergeant Olivier spoke to, and he found he was quite glad to talk to the man again, rather than having to explain everything afresh.

Sergeant Roquentin remembered his earlier conversations with Olivier very well, particularly as one of the subjects of those conversations was now lying in the undertaker's back parlour while the powers-that-be sorted out the paperwork to ship him back to wherever he had come from.

'Yes,' he agreed with Olivier, once the old policeman had set out the situation as he saw it. 'Bonnefoy, almost certainly. Probably together with that skinny little English private. But how we pin it on either one, the good Lord alone knows.'

'Not easy, I agree,' nodded Olivier. 'But if we could identify the English soldier, and lean on him a bit, he might give Bonnefoy up. What do you think?

'I think it's above my pay grade, to be honest. We'll need to get the big boys from the Sûreté involved. They know about Cadogan's murder already, of course, and I don't doubt they'll think it worth following up your lead.'

It took a number of phone calls, and a lot of waiting around, but eventually Olivier, Roquentin, and two burly men from the Sûreté were walking with purposeful steps away from the village and towards the English camp.

Sentries, identification papers, explanations, runners, more sentries, more explanations, more runners, and eventually the four men were ushered into the commanding officer's tent.

'So, gentlemen,' said the Colonel, looking up from a desk piled high with papers. 'I gather you think one of my men has been up to some funny business and caused some trouble in the village?'

'If I may,' Olivier asked deferentially. He had no rank and no official role here, but he did have excellent English, and a certain quiet authority. 'We do appreciate the difficulty this puts you under, and really we want to do nothing more than to interview one of your men, a private, who has been seen in the village on more than one occasion with one of our local villains. What your soldier has been up to is clearly no business of ours, but we were hoping he might be able to shed some light on what our own bad lad was mixed up in, and whether there was any evidence of a link between him and the murder of Jack Cadogan, one of the orderlies from your CCS.'

'Hmm.' The Colonel looked thoughtfully at the little group of sombre, serious men. 'I don't suppose you have a name for this private do you?'

'No sir,' answered Olivier. 'But, if I may, I'd suggest that he might be found among the, how shall I put it, less salubrious of your charges. Perhaps there is someone your sergeants have had reason to keep an eye on?'

'More than one, you can be sure,' the Colonel gave a wry laugh. 'Any identifying features to help single him out? No bushy moustaches or villainous scars I suppose?'

'I am afraid not, sir. The main thing that the villagers noticed about him is that he is small and skinny and seems a bit shifty.'

'Ha! Doesn't narrow it down much! Half the men in the Post Office Rifles are weedy, undernourished little runts. The London working classes, eh? Poor housing, poor diet, poor hygiene. Rats and rickets, don't you know?'

Olivier nodded. 'Much the same in Paris, sir, indeed. I don't suppose you have any ideas as to how we might identify the particular weedy little runt we're looking for?'

'I believe Sergeant-Major Williams should be able to help. Jim,' he said, turning to the adjutant who was seated to one side of the big tent. 'Could you be so good as to ask the sergeant-major to step over this way?'

'Sir,' said the adjutant crisply, stood, saluted and marched out of the tent.

'Now, gentlemen, while we're waiting for Williams, perhaps you could provide me with a few more details as to what you think has been going between your scallywag and mine?'

***

In the little clearing in the wood, everything was silent. Even the birds and the creatures that crept through the fallen leaves and straggling undergrowth seemed reluctant to move or make a sound. The man had wept and walked, screamed and shuddered, almost the whole night through. Now he sat, wrapped in the thinnest of the blankets, leaning against a tree at the edge of the glade, as far from the boys as he could manage. But his eye was drawn again and again to the rough pile of leaves and raw earth under which lay the pale body of little Jean-Baptiste. Although he had retched and retched until he felt he was turning his whole body inside out, the man could not rid himself of the slightly sweet, rusty taste of the child's blood. He wiped his sleeve across his mouth again and again and again, but it made no difference. His lips were raw, his throat burnt, he clawed at his neck, but the taste, the feel, the loathsome slippery warmth of the blood as he drank it down was lodged deep where he couldn't reach it. Occasionally a shiver shook him. His eyes were swollen with the tears he'd shed. His mouth moved and murmured constantly, 'Please no, please no more, please not again. Yes, yes, I know. Of course, I must, but please,' and so on, round and round and round.

***

Sergeant-Major Williams had listened carefully to what the four Frenchmen had had to say. A measured, thoughtful man, not given to hasty judgements, he stood silent for a while, weighing in his mind the possible candidates for this messy business from among his men.

'There's three I can think of, sir,' he said at length. 'Collins, Mason and Slater. None of them is what you'd call an out-and-out villain, but any of them would be up for handling a bit of this and that under the table, if you take my meaning, sir.'

'Thank you, Sergeant-Major, I believe I take your meaning thoroughly. How would you suggest we go about picking out our specific bad apple from this unsavoury little barrel? Is there any guidance you could give us here, do you think, Sergeant-Major?'

Colonel Forsythe had been a weekend warrior, in the Terriers, before the war. His working days had been spent running a small but thriving law practice in Deal down in Kent. He had a tendency to lead as far as he could by consultation and consensus, and was much loved for it.

'Well, sir,' the Sergeant-Major replied. 'The first thing will be to find whether any of them has left the camp, and, if they have, where they went. And then, of course, there's the question whether any of them has more spending money about their person than they ought to have. If you give me a little while with the three of them, I should be able to turn up the particular bad penny these gentlemen are seeking.'

'Well, away with you then, Sergeant-Major. Do your damnedest and then bring the fellow back here for these gentlemen to have a word with.'

The Sergeant-Major saluted and left. Olivier and the others were invited to sit by the brazier, and to have a warm rum toddy while they waited. The Colonel and the Adjutant joined them, and soon the six men were engaged in an amicable exchange of views about the Hun and the way the war was going.

In a little less than forty minutes Sergeant-Major Williams returned, with a disconsolate-looking private following on behind him.

Sidney had been no match for the Sergeant-Major's probing, knowing interrogation, and had soon come clean that he'd been peddling bits and pieces round the camp, and that he'd met up with a Frog in the village who'd sold the stuff to him.

The Colonel stood, brushed down his jacket and moved to sit down behind his desk again. All warmth and affability was gone as he looked at the sad specimen before him.

'So, man, your name and rank?'

'Slater, sir, Private Sidney Slater.'

'And you've been dealing in stolen goods and selling them on the black market, eh?'

Sidney hunched even further and hung his head, murmuring something.

'What, eh? What did you say, man? Speak up!'

'I said yes, sir.'

'Yes, sir, what?'

'Yes, I've been selling fags and such to the boys.'

'And where did you get these fags and stuff, Private Slater?'

'There was a Frenchman in the village, he had all sorts for sale.'

'And what did you give him in return, eh, Slater? Not money, I'll be bound.'

Sidney shook his head, terrified to speak, terrified to stay silent.

'Well, we'll get to the bottom of all that, you can be sure. In the meantime, though, these gentlemen want to speak to you about something even more serious than stealing supplies meant for the men you're fighting beside.'

Olivier stepped forward.

'If I may, Colonel?'

Colonel Forsythe nodded grimly.

'Private Slater, is it?' he began.

Sidney nodded. 'Yes, sir. Sidney Slater, sir, Post Office Rifles, sir.'

163

Olivier spoke quietly, almost confidingly.

'Well Private Sidney Slater, the thing is, we are looking for a murderer, and there's a very good chance that you are the murderer we're looking for.'

Sidney recoiled as if Olivier had slapped him.

'Murder, sir, honest, sir, I know nothing about no murder, truly I don't, sir.'

'But you do know something about an English medic who found you rooting around trying to get hold of drugs up at the CCS, don't you?'

'I don't know what you mean, sir.' Sidney felt hunted, cornered. That fucking, sneaking bloody orderly. What had he been saying? 'I know the man you mean, sir, of course I do, he helped me with the blisters I got from my new boots after the march up here. You ask him, he'll tell you.'

'Private Slater, I would like nothing better than to be able to ask him, but it is Jack Cadogan who was murdered. Now, man.' Olivier's tone hardened. 'When did you last see him?'

Sidney was frightened of Bonnefoy, but he was terrified of being had up on a Court Martial for murder. He'd heard enough about the hasty hearings and the firing squads. He'd rather take his chances as a thief any day. He told them all he knew - the meetings with Bonnefoy, being led off by Jack to the little yard in the village, the questions Jack had asked, how Sidney'd left him and immediately run into Bonnefoy lurking round the corner.

'I don't know nothing more, sir, honest I don't, on my mother's life.'

The Colonel said nothing. His face was blank, his lips tight, a cold anger in his eyes.

Olivier turned to Sergeant Roquentin and to the two detectives from the Sûreté.

'Enough?'

'Enough for a start, to be sure,' said the more senior of the detectives. 'I take it,' turning to the Colonel, 'that we can count on Private Slater as a witness?'

'My dear man, you can count on Slater for absolutely anything you might need. You understand that, don't you, Private? It is only your complete cooperation which is standing between you and a charge of aiding and abetting a murder. Clear?'

'Yes, sir, absolutely sir, thank you, sir.'

Sidney was led away to be delivered to the MPs.

There were handshakes and thanks all round between the small party of Frenchmen and the English Colonel and his adjutant.

'A sorry affair, and my apologies, on behalf of the British army, for our part in it,' the Colonel had said.

Olivier, the sergeant and the two detectives left and walked thoughtfully back to the village.

The policemen made their farewells and went back, a sober group, to the gendarmerie, to strategise how best to bring Bonnefoy to justice, leaving Olivier on his own at the outskirts to the village.

He thought about going home for a spell, or into the café for a drink, but neither really appealed to him. He felt curiously flat. That Jack should have been murdered over something as petty as pornography and cigarettes. What a stupid waste. And, of course, they were no closer to finding out what was happening to the missing boys.

He braced his shoulders and turned away from the village. He needed to go back to the farm.

***

The man stood in the shadow of the trees as the sun fell below the horizon and the sky grew grey. The day-long feverish struggles had left him exhausted but resolute. No more children should suffer. It was his job to make sure that they were safe, and he would carry out that duty, whatever the cost.

165

CHAPTER 17

Sunday 18th November, mid-afternoon

The motorcyclist arrived just as the major was finishing his lunch. Thanking the courier, he pushed aside the dish of tinned custard he had been about to enjoy, and opened the packet of sealed orders. He had little doubt what they would contain. With a sigh, he saw that he was right. 'Ready for imminent casualties.' The preparations were almost over then. Now it wasn't a question of if, but when - and how many. Right, then, he'd best get on with it. The custard would have to wait.

***

Murray looked up when the major stepped through the doorway. He was alone in the ward, seated beside his bed, with papers spread beside him all over the coverlet. The letters and parcels which Miranda had been sending over the past weeks and days had finally made their way to him, and he was feasting on his sister's words, and fruitcake, and chocolate.

'Anything I can do, sir?'

'No, no, that's fine, lieutenant. Just checking things over. It appears that you may not be alone here for too much longer.'

'Ah.' Murray caught the sombre undertones beneath the major's statement.

'I'll be back in a while to check your dressings. As you were, lieutenant, carry on,' and the Major ducked through the doorway into the sluice room.

Murray gathered Miranda's papers to him, and sorted them in

date order from the earliest to the most recent. He thought he'd take a chair and read them outside, in the thin light of the winter afternoon, but when he got outside and settled down, he found he could not bear to look at them. He could hardly bear to touch them, and sat, knees together, the letters on his lap, his hands just holding them enough to stop them slipping or blowing away, his eyes fixed on the orchard fence, and, beyond that, the twisted, dark horizon.

It was all foul. The stones of the farmyard were soiled and slimy and slippery. The wood of the fence-posts was mossy and rotting, the trees in the orchard had a few starved leaves clinging to the thin, bare branches. And beyond the orchard. Beyond the orchard men were dying or waiting to die. Waiting to die. Wanting to die. Wanting it all to end.

That was how Olivier found him as he came from the orchard, his scythe and rake balanced over his shoulder. The young Englishman, sitting in the gathering gloom, his face pale, his lips set.

'So, Lieutenant, how are the wounds?' asked Olivier, propping up the implements against the barn wall.

Murray seemed to contract even further into himself. He looked at Olivier with dim, dazed eyes, and it took a while for him to respond.

'The wounds? Oh, mending, mending, thank you.'

'And how is the Lieutenant?'

Murray's voice came quietly after another pause.

'Oh, also mending, thank you.'

'You look, my friend, as though a touch of cognac would not go amiss - that is, unless the good Major has said it is contra-indicated.' A slight question hung in the air.

'Thank you, sir, that's kind, and no, I don't believe Dr Carter has said anything about avoiding alcohol.' A small smile.

'Good, good. So will you come to me, or shall I bring it to you?'

'If I might join you, sir?'

'Indeed. I must just go and tidy away these tools.'

'And I must put these letters away safely.'

'Shall we say, five minutes in the farmhouse kitchen?'

***

The warmth of the small fire in the grate and the brandy - a second glass soon followed the first - had brought some colour to the Lieutenant's cheeks, but he was still sunk deep in himself.

Olivier waited quietly. If the young man wanted to speak, he would. If he didn't, then there was no need to press him.

They had not bothered to light a candle when they settled into their chairs, and now the only light was from the meagre flame in the fireplace.

'Monsieur,' Murray spoke into the silence. 'Might I ask you a question?'

'Of course, my friend, of course. Whatever you like.'

A pause, then, 'Why are we here, sir? What are we doing?'

Now Olivier paused.

'Well, I have to ask, when you say 'here' do you mean metaphysically or geographically? I am no priest, you know, young man. Just an old policeman doing the best he can.'

'Why are you and I here now, in a small farmhouse in Northern France, drinking brandy - for which many thanks - by the way, and waiting for another bloody battle?'

'Ah, well, at least a part of that I can answer. I am here, as you put it, in this small farmhouse in Northern France because this place, this village, is where I was born and schooled and grew to manhood. When my widowed mother became old and ill, I, as her only child, felt I should leave my job and come and help her through her last days. Which I did. And now I am retired from the police, but not from life, so I help out where I can, as in here, on this small farm, where Mme Blanchard manages as best she can without her husband, with hardly any stock, and with a lively, energetic, endlessly curious little boy.' He took a sip of his brandy. 'And you, young man, why are you, an Englishman, here in this small farmhouse in Northern France?'

'That, sir, is what I have been asking myself - and I am not sure I have an answer.'

'Why did you join up, if I may ask?'

'I was young, idealistic, living in a small English farming village not unlike this one. I saw the men leaving to fight - including my brother - and I saw them returning, with broken bodies, sometimes with broken minds. Or not returning at all. My brother did not return.' He sat silent for a moment and then shook himself. 'I suppose I thought I should go and do my bit.' A shrug and a wry smile.

'And now, after you have been soldiering for all these months, and been badly wounded, has that changed things?'

'Yes and no. Yes and no.'

'Which is the yes, and which is the no, may I ask?'

'The no is to this bloody stupid war, being run by bloody stupid men, for no good reason I can make out. Why ever and however it started, there can be no reason good enough to keep slaughtering young men by the tens of thousands year after year after year. I can't believe in it. I simply can't.'

'And the yes?' prompted Olivier gently.

'Ah well, the thing is, I suppose I still feel as if I should do my bit - but not for King and Country, or for the blundering buggers up at HQ putting pins in maps. Not for Horatio Bottomley and his vile *John Bull* cant.'

Murray grimaced and took a long swig at his glass.

'So who for, then?' asked Olivier.

'Oh God, for the men. For the men. For the poor benighted beggars who look to me for leadership - I can't just leave them there to muddle on if I can do anything to help them. Not that I can, you understand? But I have to try.'

Olivier reached and poured another small measure into each of their glasses.

'You are a good man, Lieutenant, and caring for the men in your command is a far, far better reason for still being here, in France, drinking brandy with an old ex-cop, than any number of flags or feathers or newspaper articles. I salute you.' And he raised his glass in a toast.

'Nothing to salute, you know,' protested Murray. 'Just a stupid beggar doing his stupid best in the middle of this whole stupid mess.'

'Ah, but, it is not always so easy to do your stupid best, to do your bit, as you say - and yet, here you are.'

They sat in silence for a while, and then gradually talked of other things - how the cow was getting on, whether there would be any nurses sent up to the CCS, whether there would a chance of some fresh meat in the village, perhaps. After a while the conversation trickled to a halt and Murray rose.

'Thank you, sir, for your kindness and your cognac. I feel now I can perhaps go and write a decent letter to my poor little sister without peppering it with 'buggers' and blasphemies. She's a good egg, and doesn't need to know anything about what it's actually like out here.'

Olivier also stood.

'Well, goodnight then, Lieutenant, and, well, good luck.'

They shook, and Murray walked carefully across the farmyard to his cold bed. He lit a candle, and settled down to weave a whimsical story around his wounding, and the CCS, and all the characters he had encountered, including, of course, the cow.

He was just pondering how to sign off when there was a sudden, wrenching cry.

***

Murray threw down his pencil, grabbed his walking stick and

171

made his way as fast as he could out into the yard.

Madeleine was there, crouched in the middle of the courtyard, Olivier kneeling beside her.

'What's happened? Is Madame alright? Has she fallen? Is she hurt?'

Olivier looked up at him, his face ghostly in the light of the waxing moon.

'Worse, much worse. Little Alex is gone.'

'Gone! Gone? I don't understand. What do you mean, gone?'

The major had left his room and joined the small group in the yard. He put a hand on Murray's arm.

'Steady, lad, let's not make things worse for Madame. Do you think,' turning to Olivier, 'that Madame might be persuaded to come indoors and tell us what she knows, so that we can do what we can to help?'

Between them, Olivier and the major supported Madeleine back into the farmhouse and sat her down beside the fireplace. The major fetched his whisky and poured a small tot for Madeleine.

'It's medicine, Madame,' he told her gravely.

Madeleine sniffed at the glass and grimaced, then tossed the drink back in one go. She gasped a little and then looked at the three men anxiously gathered round her. Olivier spoke.

'Can you tell us as much as you can about what has happened, so that we can find Alex and bring him home to you?'

She shuddered, and it almost seemed as though she would break down again, but she drew back from the terror coursing through her, and forced herself to tell Olivier and the others as much as she could.

'Alex was playing with you this morning, Olivier,' she began. Olivier nodded. 'Then, after he'd had his lunch and a nap, I took him into the village this afternoon and left him with Maman while I went to see if there was anything more I could do for Anne-Marie. I didn't stay long with her - just long enough to do a bit of cleaning and tidying, really - she's shut in on herself, poor woman. She won't talk, just carries on as if everything were the same as usual. It's almost as if little Paul had never existed.' Madeleine gave a small shrug and sank into silence.

Olivier waited quietly, and then prompted, 'After leaving Madame Mardel, where did you go?'

'Why, I went to my mother's to collect Alex!' Madeleine sounded almost indignant. Where else would she have gone? What would she have been doing except fetching her child home?

'And when you got to your mother's?'

'I couldn't see Alex outside - he usually plays with pebbles and things in the road, making them into trains, or fleets of pirate ships, or any number of things.' She looked up at the men with something like a smile. 'He has whole worlds inside his head, you know?' Another pause, and then, 'Well, he wasn't outside, so I went in, and Maman was sitting dozing in her chair. I thought perhaps Alex had got tired and that she'd put him to bed. I crept across the room and pushed back the curtain round Maman's bed. It was all neatly made, and no, Alex wasn't there. So I woke Maman.'

'And what did your mother tell you?' Olivier nudged her along.

'She said that Alex was at Monsieur Rivière's house. That Monsieur Rivière had come along and met Alex playing in the street and had asked him whether he'd like to go to his house and look at some of the story books he has. Alex asked Maman, and Maman said that was fine. I thought it was very kind of Monsieur Rivière. He has looked so tired and ill recently. I thought it was a good sign that he was taking an interest in life again. This war, and the memories it brought back, have been hard on him, I think.'

Olivier was silent.

'Anyway, I got together Alex's things, thanked Maman, and went to Monsieur Riviére's house to fetch Alex. But,' Madeleine faltered, then went on. 'The house was locked, gentlemen, the windows shuttered. No lights, no sign at all of anyone. I knocked, of course, but no-one came. I went round to the back door, but the garden was all tangled and overgrown. You could hardly reach the door for weeds and brambles. I did, though. I got to the door, and knocked, but there was nothing. It just sounded, I don't know, empty.'

All of a sudden, the words tumbled out of Madeleine in a rush.

'I was a bit, well, confused, but I wasn't really worried. I thought Maman had got things slightly wrong again - it wouldn't be the first time - and perhaps Monsieur Rivière had taken Alex to the café, or to visit the priest, or perhaps even here, back home. But he wasn't in the café, and he wasn't at the priest's house, and he's nowhere here. Do you know what I think, gentlemen?' Madeleine looked round at three anxious men. 'I think that monster has attacked poor Monsieur Rivière and stolen my Alex.'

She flung her head in her hands, and her shoulders shook, but she didn't make a sound.

Murray leant forward and tentatively laid a hand on her arm. He had no words.

The major looked questioningly at Olivier, but Olivier seemed to have withdrawn deep into himself.

Perhaps, he was thinking, perhaps it was the case that Mathieu Rivière had not been attacked by the monster. Perhaps Mathieu Rivière was the monster.

CHAPTER 18

19th November, dawn till midnight

He'd come from the woods at first light. He'd watched all morning, knowing the right time would come.

Once the ex-policeman and the child had gone in to the house for their lunch, he'd waited in the little orchard by the farmhouse. He thought to catch the boy's attention when he came out to play in the afternoon, and promise him new playmates up in the woods. He'd always seemed lonely and at a bit of a loose end unless Olivier was there to keep him entertained. He remembered Olivier from long ago, when everything was different. He'd always been kind and patient, even as a boy.

The grass was long and damp, even in the thin afternoon sun, and the cold seeped through the soles of his boots, chilling him. Then the farmhouse door opened, and little Alex tumbled out, quickly followed by his mother. They were clearly off into the village together. No matter, he could guess where they were going, and in a way it would be even better there. He turned and made his way, silently, invisibly, through the fields and down the pathways, until he reached a spot where he could easily keep an eye out for the boy, without being observed by anyone passing by.

The village was full of harsh noises and hurrying people. Soldiers dashed past in twos and threes, shouting and joking with each other, in a fever of anxious gaiety. Everyone knew something big was coming, and each was masking their terror in their own way. He watched their wide, shining eyes and the rough horseplay with which they greeted each other, and sensed their desperate fear. It was getting urgent, he must make sure the children were kept safe.

He didn't have too long to wait. Alex and his mother arrived at the old woman's house and knocked on the low wooden door. A quick exchange of words at the doorstep, and then Madeleine went off, while Alex was swallowed up into the darkness of his grandmother's tiny cottage. He knew it wouldn't be long now. The old woman, with her swollen ankles and fading eyesight, wouldn't be able to cope with the boy's vivid energy. A few minutes, at most, and he'd be sent out to amuse himself in the street.

He didn't go across to little Alex the moment he appeared. He waited until the first rush of eager exploration was over, and the child was clearly beginning to wonder what he could do next.

'Hello, Alex, are you waiting for Maman to come back?'

'Hello, Monsieur. Yes, Maman's gone to see Madame Mardel. Madame Mardel is very sad at the moment, she says.'

'And what about you, Alex, are you sad at the moment?'

Alex thought for a moment.

'No, not really sad, but I wish -' He paused.

'What do you wish, little one?' The big man said kindly, crouching down beside the boy.

'I wish things were like they were before, before the Boches came. They've made everything horrid.'

The man smiled.

'In my house I have storybooks with pictures, stories of beautiful, exciting things, ships and dragons, pirates and princes. Would you like to see them? They might make things seem less horrid.'

Alex was entranced at the idea. Picture books. He hadn't seen many, and mostly they were of Bible stories, but he loved the way they were bright and strange and different.

'Let's go and ask your grandmother, shall we?' asked the man.

The grandmother had been flustered when he'd knocked on the

door and gone into the house with the boy.

'Well, of course, Monsieur, that's extremely kind of you, if you're sure that won't be too much trouble. Alex,' she'd said, turning to the boy, 'you must be very good now. No running about and shouting.' She looked up into the man's face. 'He is a good boy, though, you know, a lovely, clever boy.'

'I know he is, Madame,' he'd said gravely. 'I can see it. Please don't worry. He'll be no trouble, I am certain, and I'll be sure to keep him safe.'

And as easily as that it was done. The grandmother had gone back to her knitting or sewing or whatever, and he had taken little Alex's hand in his and walked away with him down the street.

He'd thought at first that he might indeed take him back to his house and show him some of the picture books he still had on the shelves, the jetsam left beached by the receding tide of his former life, but then he'd decided it'd be best to get straight back to the little glade before dark, so that he could introduce Alex to his new friends.

***

Murray had stayed in the kitchen with Madeleine while Olivier and the major took torches and searched every inch of the farm, every cupboard and cranny, outbuilding and shed. The boy was nowhere there.

'I think,' said the major, 'that the time has come to call in reinforcements. It's not like the child to wander off, and what with everything that's been going on, well, we'd best just make sure he's found, eh?'

Olivier was in complete agreement.

Leaving the major in charge of the CCS, and Lieutenant Coverdale taking care of Madeleine, he strode urgently down to the village and knocked at the firmly closed door of the gendarmerie. He had no idea how late it was - there was a waxing moon just visible in the overcast

177

sky - but late or early, it was time to rouse the village, or at least the village policeman.

Sergeant Roquentin answered the hammering at the door, his hair tousled and his baggy woollen long johns visible under the coat he had hastily slung round his shoulders.

Seeing Olivier, he stepped back. 'Come in, monsieur. What's happened?' The sergeant knew Olivier well enough by this time to be sure it was no light matter which had brought him hammering on his door in the dead of night.

'It's Alex Blanchard, Mme Blanchard's little boy, he's gone missing, and with the number of little boys who've been disappearing of late, I thought that we'd best get some sort of search party organised as soon as possible and see if we can't pick up his traces.'

Sergeant Roquentin leant back against the tall desk which divided the front room of the police station from the office, and, beyond, his living quarters.

'You're right, of course, Monsieur Verger. You have much more experience of these matters. But, to be honest, as things stand, I'm not sure quite how much we can do. I don't want to alarm the women and children, and there are very few able-bodied men left here now. But yes, let's go quietly, gather who we can, and see what we can discover.'

It wasn't much, and they didn't find much.

Such men as they could bring together into a search party were sent to look systematically through the village and as far they could go along the towpath, to see if they could pick up any hint of where the boy might have got to.

Olivier himself went on his own to Mathieu Rivière's house. He hadn't mentioned his suspicions to anybody. If he was wrong, and the old man heard what he'd been accused of, well, it would finish him off entirely. Although Olivier had seen little of him in recent months, he'd heard enough to know that the man was struggling badly with the effects of this new war. The last war with the Germans had almost destroyed him. He didn't need further torments added to everything he already suffered.

But if, just possibly, it was Rivière who was responsible for these children disappearing, there might, perhaps, be a clue as what was happening somewhere locked up in his darkened house.

***

Alex wasn't unhappy. He liked walking along in the dark well enough. But he was a little puzzled. He looked up at the man treading quietly beside him.

'Excuse me, monsieur, but I thought we were going to go to your house to look at the books with pictures?'

'And so we will, little one, so we will, but not just yet. First I'd like to take you to a special place, where you can meet some new play-mates.'

'Is it far, monsieur?' Alex was beginning to feel a little tired, and it seemed awfully late to be out and not at home in his bed.

'Not far at all, my boy, not far at all. Just up this lane, round the corner, and up that hill, there, see, into the woods.' He looked down. He could feel the little boy begin to drag against him. 'Would you like me to carry you? And perhaps I can tell you one of those stories at the same time as we walk along? It won't have pictures, but perhaps you can make the pictures in your head, eh?'

And so the old man lifted up the child, and carried him cradled against his shoulder, and as they walked he murmured stories of princes and heroes from long ago. Alex nodded against his shoulder, the words weaving brilliant images behind his gently closing eyelids.

***

At first it seemed to Olivier that he was on a fool's errand. The house stood dark and austere on the outskirts of the village, slightly

179

aloof, as befitted a schoolmaster's house. No lights shone from any of the windows. He knocked, as Madeleine had done. No answer. He had expected none. He went round the back, as Madeleine had done, and followed the path of crushed and broken weeds she had made to reach the back door. He knocked again. Again no answer. But now he looked around. He needed a rock, a stone, something to break the little glass window set in the door. He couldn't see anything. With a sigh - it was something he'd done before, but never without anxiety, and the last time had been several years ago - tightening his jacket around his arm, he set his elbow against the little window, made a fist, and slammed against the fist as hard as he could with his other hand. The glass shattered. For a moment he stood entirely still. Had anyone heard? The night was silent, apart from the constant muffled thudding of guns, far down the line on the left.

Gingerly, Olivier knocked the shards of glass from the window frame, reached in, found the key to the door resting in the lock, turned it, and pushed the door open. It was utterly dark in the house, and smelled musty, with a slight undertone of mouse droppings. He felt along the wall. A gas mantle, with matches lying on a shelf just below it. He struck a match, lifted the glass chimney, turned the gas on and lit the wick. Replacing the chimney, he looked around him as the light rose and steadied. He felt very strange, to be an intruder here, where he had once, on a very few, privileged occasions, been a guest, one of a select few.

He looked around for a light, and saw an oil lamp, half full, on the kitchen table. Reaching for the matches again, he quickly lit the lamp, and began to explore the silent house. He had no idea what he was looking for, but he knew he'd recognise it when he saw it.

***

They reached the glade. The hammock, with its stiffened stains, gleamed dimly in the weak moonlight. Mathieu went to lay Alex in

180

it, but as he bent down the boy awoke, looking round him with eyes of wonder.

'But this is where Papa is! This is where we're all going to live after the war is over.'

Mathieu had no idea what the boy was talking about, but his heart jolted at the tone of the child's eager voice.

He led him away from the hammock and towards the ashes of the campfire.

'Sit here, child, and tell me what you mean while I get a fire started.'

The man reached for twigs from the bundle of kindling he had stored in the lean-to, and fetched a blanket at the same time to wrap round the little boy.

Soon there were flames to warm them, and water set to heat over the fire, while Mathieu and Alex shared the blanket, and gnawed at the end of a loaf which Mathieu had had in his pocket, and which he'd divided between them.

'How do you know this is where your Papa is, my boy?' The man asked gently. And so the whole story came tumbling out, the story which Alex had heard so many times as his mother tucked him into bed and talked to him of his father and showed him the animals he had carved.

'And so,' he finished, 'once the war is over, Maman and I will come and live in the woods with Papa, and sit quietly and watch the animals play.'

Mathieu's cheeks were wet with tears.

'That is quite right, dear boy, quite right. Here in the woods, with loved ones around you, this is the only place you can be happy now.' And he drew the boy closer to him. They were both sleepy with the warmth of the fire, and the comfort of bread and a hot drink.

Time enough, Mathieu thought, lying down beside the dozing boy. Time enough in the morning. And so they settled down to sleep by the dying embers of the fire, the man with one arm around the boy.

His other hand rested on the hilt of his knife.

***

Olivier had been through the whole house, from attic to cellar. He had begun to form a picture of the man who was Mathieu Rivière. He sat at the mahogany dining table where it was clear that Rivière usually sat, and mulled everything over. It all felt extremely strange. For a start, he wasn't used to thinking of Monsieur Rivière as anything but Monsieur Rivière. He'd known he had a first name of course, but the idea of using it was totally foreign to him - he could just as easily have called his mother Juliette. Somehow he had to get a grip on his thinking - it seemed to be sliding around in his head, stopping him looking at things directly. He reached into his pocket and drew out a notebook and a pen. Immediately he felt slightly better. Method, that's what he needed. Even if he wasn't going to be writing a report, he could still use the processes which had stood him in such good stead over his career. He tore three sheets of paper out of the notebook and laid them in a row in front of him on the table. On one he wrote THE PAST, on the second WHAT I KNOW, and on the third QUESTIONS.

'Well, I can deal with the past relatively straightforwardly, I believe.' He found himself murmuring aloud, his voice sounding thin in the huge silence of the empty house. He noted down a series of questions fairly rapidly, before setting about supplying the answers as accurately as he could.

When did M. Rivière first come here?

How old was he?

How old was I?

What was he like?

And then the answers.

Mid-to-late 1870s

24, 25??

About 15?

And then Olivier paused. He felt that somewhere in the answer to this question lay the answer to everything. He stood and strode to the where the back door still stood ajar, and, gazing out into the night, carefully lit his pipe as he let the memories settle.

Mathieu Rivière had come to the village as the new schoolmaster. To the older boys, coming up to their last few months and years of school, he had seemed like a breath of fresh air. Monsieur Simon, the retiring master, had seemed as old as Methuselah to the boys, and the lessons he gave were as dull and dry as ships biscuits - providing some kind of nourishment, without doubt, but hard to choke down. Monsieur Rivière, on the other hand, Monsieur Rivière made the whole world come alive.

Biology lessons were walks through the fields and along the canals, collecting plants and insects, fish and small animals, all to be brought back to the classroom to be examined and discussed, each neatly categorised so that the random world of the children became systematised and coherent.

History was maps laid out on the schoolroom floor, with toy soldiers moving across this way and that, and heterogeneous farm animals and zoo creatures dragooned into playing their part, following the trade routes - sometimes marching implausibly across the sea.

And literature, ah, literature, that was what Olivier had loved best. The books that Monsieur Rivière read aloud, while the boys lay sprawled at their desks or stretched out across the floor, their minds carried away to far lands and distant times, until they could almost see the mountains where Le Cid fought off the Moors, or step behind the dank castle walls where the man in the iron mask was held a prisoner. Sights, sounds, smells, Monsieur Rivière brought them all alive with the way he read, and the way he talked about what he was reading - the characters, the places, the authors - why they had written as they did, and why they should be honoured for what they had given to the world.

It was literature that had first brought him to this house when he'd been what, sixteen? Seventeen? He had written an essay on Baudelaire which had pleased Monsieur Rivière greatly, and he and another two or three favoured few were invited to visit Monsieur Rivière at his home one Sunday afternoon for some coffee and cake, to talk about writers and writing. It was then that Monsieur Rivière had led him from Baudelaire to the American writer whose work Baudelaire so admired, and much of which he had translated. And Monsieur Rivière had lent him a copy of Edgar Allan Poe's Murders in the rue Morgue. What a book! The imagination, the logic. It was probably that book as much as anything which had led him to become a policeman. And now here he was, investigating the man who had set him on that path. Olivier grunted at the irony of it, knocked out his pipe against the kitchen window sill, and walked back to the dining table and his notes.

He jotted down his memories of Rivière as a teacher - and that is what he had been, a true teacher, generous, iconoclastic, widely-read, enthusiastic. That was the Rivière of the past. But what had he learnt, what had he seen, of the Rivière of the present in his careful exploration of the house? What, to be precise, did he know of Mathieu Rivière now?

He went through the house in his mind, room by room, from top to bottom. The cellar had had very little in it - a few sticks of broken furniture, a half-dozen bottles of wine, the remnants of a stack of logs. Of the rooms on the ground floor, the reception rooms were clearly barely used, apart from the dining room, which looked as if Rivière had adopted it as his study. There were books on the shelves, and a stack of newspapers in one corner. Olivier got up to look at them more closely. They were brittle and yellowed. The most recent dated to September 1914 - over three years old. And it was the same all over the house. The clocks still whirred and chimed, but the time they told was somehow distorted, warped.

The rooms on the upper floors all had the look of having been

184

abandoned years before, apart from Rivière's bedroom. There clothes tumbled from the cupboard and the chests of drawers, some neatly folded or carefully arranged on hangers, others in a heap on the floor, clean and soiled all mixed together. The bed had been slept in. The sheets were rumpled and grey. Olivier had not touched them, but they looked stiff with grease and dirt. The linen had not been changed for a very long time.

Olivier turned to his notes and wrote underneath QUESTIONS, What happened to the housekeeper?

In the bathroom, brown stains in the sink and bath. Rivière's shaving kit stood on a shelf above the handbasin, a rusting razor-blade in the safety razor, and the bristles of the shaving brush brittle and dry.

On the sheet marked WHAT I KNOW he wrote, R. not taking care of himself, hasn't for a long time. And on the sheet marked QUESTIONS, What changed? When?

He took his empty pipe out of his pocket and sucked on it thoughtfully. He knew he had overlooked something. There was something he had seen somewhere upstairs that was tugging at his mind. He picked up the lantern and went back up to the landing, then wandered slowly into the bathroom. Mmm, not there. What about the bedroom? He stood in the doorway and looked over everything, the piles of clothes, the grimy sheets, and then stepped right into the room and gazed around. Yes, of course! The photo. He hadn't really looked at it before, but now he went over to the dressing table, and plucked it from where it was wedged between the mirror and the frame. It was a smallish photo, hand-tinted, a picture of seven young men in the military uniform of the Second Empire - red képis, short blue jackets and baggy red trousers. He carried the photo down with him to the dining room, so that he could see it properly and study it more closely.

They looked so young, these soldiers. A couple of them had thin moustaches. The others looked as if they'd barely begun to shave. They were all grinning at the cameraman, posed with their arms around each other's shoulders. A group of friends. Going to war? Coming back from war? On leave? There was no clue to the occasion. Then Olivier noticed some marks on the faces of the young men. It looked as though the faces of four of them had been crossed out in pencil, and another two in pen, with a fine nib, and in red ink. The marks had faded with time and were almost invisible, but yes, six of the seven had been crossed out.

Olivier peered more closely. The seventh, was that a very young Monsieur Rivière? He was fairly sure it was. But what did the photo mean? Who were these soldier-boys? Why had their faces been crossed out so carefully and precisely?

He drew the notepaper headed QUESTIONS towards him. Who is in the photo? He wrote. Who crossed out the six men? Why?

He leaned back and heaved a great sigh. He was fairly sure that there was something deeply wrong with Mathieu Rivière, but what, and whether it was linked to the disappearance of the boys, and of little Alex, he had no idea. He needed something more. But what? And from where?

He wondered how the villagers had got on in their search. Drawing out his pocket-watch, he saw it was close to midnight. Time to get back to the gendarmerie and see if there was any news. He stood and stretched, and as he dropped his arms he knocked the pieces of paper with his notes onto the floor. A muttered oath, and he knelt to retrieve them. There was something odd there, under the table. He reached and brought the light down. There was a little clump of reddish brown soil and some fragments of dead leaves. It didn't look like anything that could have come from Rivière's garden, nor from the street outside. It was brown earth from somewhere that Rivière had been walking which had come off from his boots as he sat at the table. Where had Rivière been? And what had he been doing?

Olivier carefully tore another sheet from his notebook, and gathered up the soil and leaves, folding it over so that none of it would fall out. He put the little packet in his pocket. Now he just had to find the patch of earth it had come from. And how he was to do that, he had simply no idea.

**

The search party had found nothing, and the men scattered, dispirited, to their various homes. As he trudged back to the farm to bear the gloomy tidings of no news, he was startled to hear plane after plane flying low overhead into the black night. He could hear gunfire from the German lines as the planes flew over. Whatever was going on, it wasn't good.

CHAPTER 19

Alex woke before dawn. The wood was strangely silent. No birds stirring, no rustlings in the undergrowth. The man was fast asleep beside him. They had both been woken several times in the night by the steady drone of aeroplanes flying close by and low, and by the rattle and thud of German guns meeting them as they crossed the line. In the end the man had carried Alex across into the shelter of the lean-to, and had covered them over with as many blankets as he had to keep them warm and to muffle the noise. And so they'd finally fallen into a deep sleep, Alex's head resting on the man's broad chest. And now the man slept on, and Alex, unmoving, opened his eyes, and looked into the grey shadows of the glade. It was entirely still here, with no sound but the man's steady breathing. He wriggled very quietly out of the blankets and sat at the edge of the shelter. The birds and the little creatures had been frightened into silence by the aeroplanes and the guns. They'd creep back later, he was sure. He wanted to show Maman this place and to ask her if this was where Papa would come when all the fighting was over. He turned his head and looked over at the man. He seemed so tired. Alex didn't want to wake him. He'd come back with Maman and they could bring the man some bread and milk for his breakfast.

Quietly, quietly Alex stood up and crept to the edge of the glade, looking for the path they had followed when they came through the wood. It was difficult in the dark. There wasn't a glimmer of light in the sky, only the distant flashes of big guns far away. He groped his way down the path and set off for his home.

***

No-one had slept at the farm. Olivier and Madeleine had sat to-gether in the farmhouse kitchen, the smallest of fires set in the grate to ward off the damp chill. He had told her of the search in the village, and of his suspicions about the schoolmaster. After that, there had seemed nothing more to say, and so they had stayed sitting silently on either side of the table, waiting for the night to end so that they could look for Alex again.

While the new orderlies tossed and turned trying to get comfort-able overhead in the hayloft, Murray had lain wide awake alone on the empty ward, listening to the planes overhead, and to the clanks and moans of machinery moving up the road outside the farm. And somewhere in all this upheaval was Madame's little boy. He thought of Miranda when she had been Alex's age, and his heart ached. For her, for him, for them all.

Major Carter knew exactly what the constant flights of aeroplanes portended. It had been spelled out at the briefing meeting at head-quarters. The planes were to divert the enemy's attention and to mask the noise of the tanks and the troops as they were brought into posi-tion. As soon as the sky lightened, the attack would begin. He sat at his desk and put thoughts of the missing little boy to one side. Draw-ing the piles of requisitions towards him, he checked through again to make sure that he had everything he'd need in the coming hours.

***

It wasn't easy finding his way home. The shapes were all different in the dark. Gradually, though, Alex made his way down the hill and across the fields, taking some wrong turnings but all the time mov-ing towards the village and the farm. As he crept closer to the farm, he realised that there were men and movement everywhere. Files of soldiers walked silently, some with cigarettes cupped in their hands so that the glow of the tip would not show. Others stood or sat, wait-ing for orders. And slowly, across the fields and along the paths and roads, crept the tanks, hunched monsters lumbering forwards.

Alex slid behind hedges and along ditches, keeping out of sight of the men, wanting only to get home and find his mother.

It was still dark when he reached the familiar outlines of the farm. He avoided the thronged road, and wriggled his way around until he could slip unseen into the orchard. From there, over the gate, across the yard, to the front door. He stopped for a moment. He hoped Grandmother had told Maman that she had said it was alright for him to go with the man, and that Maman wouldn't be too cross that he had been out all night. He squared his slender shoulders, turned the handle and pushed against the door as quietly as he could. He didn't want to wake Maman if she was still sleeping.

But she wasn't sleeping. She was sitting at the table, opposite the front door, watching the door with wide, terrified eyes as it slowly nudged open. Then she saw her son, pale, hesitant, his face and clothes filthy with dust and leaves. Madeleine leapt from her chair and threw herself down on her knees in front of the boy, pulling him to her, stroking his back, stroking his hair, touching his cheeks, and all the while murmuring, almost as if not to wake herself from a dream, 'You're here, you're safe, you're home. I love you. You're home again, my darling. You're safe.'

Olivier watched the scene in wonder. He very much wanted to know what had happened, where Alex had been, how he had got home, but now was not the time to speak. He stood and walked to the fireplace, loading logs into the grate until the fire was blazing, and putting a kettle on the hob to boil. Then he stepped quietly to the major's room and knocked on the door.

'Come,' Major Carter looked up from his desk as Olivier pushed his door slightly ajar and peeked in just enough to say, 'The boy has come back. I'm making coffee,' and then closed the door quietly again.

The major methodically screwed the lid back on his fountain pen, laid it down on the desk, and then stepped out into the kitchen. Madame and her child were sitting close to the fire. Alex was chattering

191

excitedly, while Madeleine held and stroked him, almost laughing, almost crying. The major crossed the kitchen and went to the door. He needed to tell the lieutenant. As he opened the door and stepped into the yard he saw that there was an ominous pallor in the sky to the east. It wouldn't be long now.

Hurriedly he stepped across the courtyard and brought the news to Murray. Together the two men hastened back to the farmyard kitchen, sharing hesitant smiles. Perhaps things would go well after all.

***

Mathieu was bereft, furious with himself, inconsolable. He had failed, failed utterly, failed unforgivably. He had let the lovely little child slip back into the hell below when he should have kept him safe. And yes, he would have kept him safe, if he had done what he was supposed to do, and not been beguiled by the boy to sit by the fire and tell stories. He hurried over to the little group of graves at the edge of the clearing.

'I am so sorry, my boys, so sorry. But you are still here, and I will look after you. Later, I promise, soon, I will bring you more friends.' And he sat amongst them, patting the soil, shaking his head and muttering.

***

It was nearly full dawn when the attack started.

One minute there had been silence, and then suddenly, for miles in each direction, there were whistles, gunfire, and the throaty roar of three battalions of tanks moving forward into battle. Men shouted, men cried out in fear and exhilaration, asses brayed, horses neighed and screamed. Guns thundered, rattled, coughed. Shells and grenades exploded. The tanks, infantrymen beside them, bayonets fixed,

192

moved inexorably on.

***

The major consulted his pocket watch. 6:20. Very impressive.

He left Murray in the kitchen, sitting with Madeleine, Olivier and the little boy, and strode briskly across the courtyard to the Clearing Station, shouting to rouse the orderlies as he went. Entering the darkness of the ward, he struck a match and started lighting the lanterns which hung along the central beam of the barn.

'Come on lads and lasses, up now and to your posts. It won't be long at all until we're needed.'

***

In the farmhouse, Olivier was speaking earnestly to Madeleine.

'We have to know where he went. Rivière is insane. It must be him who is taking the boys. He has to be stopped.'

'No, no,' Madeleine was adamant. 'I don't want to hear any more. Alex is home safe. That's all that matters. He's here and here I will keep him until this madness is over.'

'But Madeleine -'

'No, not another word. I won't listen.'

She drew Alex closer to her as he sat on her knee, and gazed defiantly at the old policeman.

'Maman,' said the child. 'It was very nice in the woods, the monsieur was very kind. Do you think that is where Papa will be when the soldiers have stopped fighting?'

'Oh, Alex, my darling boy,' Madeleine buried her face against her son's head, resting her lips against the precious curve at the nape of his neck.

Olivier asked gently, 'Did you see any other boys when you were in the woods, Alex?'

Madeleine looked daggers, but Alex answered happily.

'No, I didn't see them. I think they must have been asleep. Monsieur said there were lots of other boys there for me to play with.'

Olivier paused thoughtfully. Perhaps he had been wrong. Perhaps the boys were safe. Perhaps Rivière had simply kidnapped them for some strange reason of his own, and was keeping them prisoner up there. If so, it was more than time that they were rescued. They couldn't stay safe for much longer.

He listened as the noise of battle roiled beyond the door.

Suddenly an idea occurred to him.

'Alex, would you mind taking off your jumper?'

Both Alex and Madeleine looked at him in surprise.

'Do you think he's hurt?' Madeleine's voice was low and troubled.

'No, no, not at all. I just want to check something.'

Alex pulled his jumper over his head and handed it across the table to the old policeman. Olivier laid it carefully on the table, and brought over two candles, lighting them carefully before placing them at the head and foot of the jumper. Madeleine and the boy watched in baffled silence. Olivier bent close to the jumper, and examined it carefully. Then he reached into his pocket, and drew the packet of soil and leaves he had collected from Mathieu Rivière's dining-room floor. He laid it beside the jumper and unfolded it carefully.

'Well, I'll be damned! Forgive me, Madeleine,' he apologised hastily. 'It's just that the clever fellow was absolutely right after all. Every contact leaves a trace!'

'I have absolutely no idea what you're talking about, Olivier,' rebuked Madeleine, reaching for a shawl to wrap around her son.

'This soil, you see, this brown earth on Alex's jumper, it's the same as the soil I took from Rivière's carpet. I'd be willing to wager if I had a microscope I'd be able to demonstrate that they're identical.'

'And? Earth is earth is earth. And the good Lord knows there's enough of it round here. And more of it, I don't doubt, after today.'

'No, Madeleine, really not at all. There are so many different types of earth. You know that's true, don't you?'

She nodded reluctantly.

'But these two earths are the same. So if we find where Alex got this soil on the jumper, we will, I am prepared to swear, find Monsieur Rivière and the missing boys!'

'And how do you propose to do that? There is a battle going on just outside our door!'

But as they paused and listened, they realised that the sounds had changed.

Tanks and men were no longer pouring past. The gunfire was more distant. Olivier went to the door and opened it.

It was now full day, and the sight that met his eyes astonished him.

The yard was almost empty, apart from walking wounded and ambulances arriving at the CCS. The soldiers, the great guns, the lumbering tanks all seemed to have disappeared. There was the sound of fighting over the horizon. But nothing to be seen.

'I'm just going to see what's happening,' he explained to Madeleine, and, closing the door to keep the little family safe and warm, he went across and into the great barn. Here there was noise, and crowds, and hurrying feet. He looked around. Major Carter was busy with a badly wounded man, wrapping bandages as best he could around a face that looked half shot away.

'A Blighty one for you, my boy, that's for sure. Home to your mother and your best girl, and plenty of best bitter, I've no doubt.' He put a smile into his voice. The boy was blinded, and, if he survived, he wouldn't have a face that any girl would want to kiss.

'Stretcher bearers,' he called. 'Take this lucky lad back to Base, please, quick as you can.'

'Sir!' And the boy was carried out, to whatever future awaited him.

The major looked up and saw Olivier watching him.

'So, all happy on the home front, now, eh? Boy back in one piece and Mama killing fatted calves? Not there's any of those to be found these days, eh?' The major joked, his eyes roaming over the casualties sitting, lying, standing in front of him, to see who next needed him most urgently.

'Something like that,' replied Olivier. 'And what's the news from here? It all seems oddly empty outside.'

'It seems,' the major answered cautiously, 'that there has been a breakthrough. The tanks have crossed the Hindenburg Line and are keeping going. Several miles, one of the men was saying. Perhaps those confounded clattering contraptions will be the saving of us after all, and everyone can tidy up and go home.'

'Ah major, what a blissful thought. Too blissful to be believed, I fear. But,' Olivier turned, 'I must leave you to your labours. You are much needed still. Do you know, by chance, where Lieutenant Coverdale might be?'

'Well yes, I believe he's in the sluice room winding bandages.'

'Thank you, dear major, thank you.'

Olivier made his way past the crowd of groaning men, and went into the sluice room, where Murray was busy turning the handle on a bandage-winder, holding the cloth taut so that it was wound tight and flat.

'Lieutenant, do you think you could be spared a moment? I have an urgent task for you, if you're up for it.'

'Of course, sir, whatever I can do. I feel utterly useless here, with these brave boys coming in, and me not able to do a damned thing to ease their pain.'

'I believe little Alex knows where the rest of the little boys are, and can take us to them, but Madeleine is very reluctant - quite understandably. I can't but feel it's urgent, the boys need to be found and helped, and Alex is the only one who can guide us. Could you, do you think, act as our escort? It might reassure Madeleine a little.'

'I'll just ask the major, and if he allows it, then I'll be honoured, sir.'

And so it was that, just a few minutes later, Olivier, Madeleine, Alex and Murray made their way out of the farmyard and along the road, walking steadily away from the war and towards the woods.

CHAPTER 20

20th November, mid-morning onwards

Mathieu heard them before he saw them. Alex calling, excited, happy. Lower voices, men, two, perhaps three. No, definitely two. And a woman's voice murmuring. Their feet scuffed and crunched through the fallen leaves as they came closer. He stayed where he was, sitting in the centre of the little group of children he had saved, patting the mounds of earth and murmuring reassurances to them.

'Don't worry, don't worry, you're safe, you're safe. I'll not let you come to harm.'

It was Olivier who saw him first as he stepped into the glade. He stood quite still, and looked at the man he had so revered.

Mathieu Rivière was filthy, unshaven, his eyes sunken, his cheeks hollow, and a wild, hectic light in his eyes.

'Don't come nearer, Olivier. Stay there. You've always been a good boy. Don't frighten the children. Keep away.'

'What children, Monsieur Rivière? Where are they hiding?'

'Why here, of course, here, all safe together.' And Mathieu gestured to the eight small mounds around him. 'Can't you hear them giggling? They think you're really funny, standing there looking so stern. And who are these? Why, it's little Alex! I thought I'd lost you, boy. How wonderful you've come back. Come here, come here.' He gestured to the child, but Madeleine took him in her arms and held him firm.

'He's not coming anywhere near you again, you foul, vile, crazy man.'

Murray moved forward, limping heavily after the long walk, and stood between Madeleine and the crouching man.

'What now, sir?' Murray asked Olivier.

'Well,' the old policeman spoke slowly. 'I fear we know what has become of those poor little lads. It's clear the man is mad, but, none-theless, he must be brought in and handed to the police. Eight little boys. Eight boys, what a tragedy. So sad, so very, very sad.' He paused. 'But you don't need to stay, my dear lieutenant, nor you, Madeleine - and especially not little Alex. This is no place for you. Go back to the farm and stay in the farmhouse until I get back. I'll escort Monsieur Rivière to the gendarmerie, and then I'll come and join you.' His eyes were moist and clouded with tears. 'So many broken lives. Will it nev-er end?'

Madeleine, Alex held firmly on her hip, turned to walk back down the path. Murray gave one final glance round the clearing, and caught sight of the little wooden hutch, with a pile of leaves and grass lying scattered in front of it. He strode over and looked down. The rabbit, confident that yet more food was on its way, hopped out of the corner to greet him.

'Excellent,' said the lieutenant with a smile. 'Rabbit stew. The boys'll be all the better for that. The major will be delighted.' He reached down, lifted the lid of the cage, picked up the rabbit and snapped its neck.

Swinging the rabbit by its legs, he hurried down the path after Madeleine and the boy, keen to catch up with them and keep them company.

***

Olivier stood silently for a long while, then walked over and sat down beside the troubled figure of his old schoolmaster. He looked carefully round the glade. He saw the lean-to with its tattered pile of blankets, the ashes of the fire with the blackened metal pot beside it. The empty rabbit hutch. The hammock, stiff and dark with layers of dried blood. Finally he looked at the eight small graves, covered with brown earth and fragments of dried leaves. The same earth, the same leaves he had found under the table at Mathieu Rivière's house.

The old man was watching him, shaking lightly, a small, hopeful smile tugging at his lips. 'I knew you'd understand. You were always so quick, so sympathetic. I couldn't have them hurt again. They're safe here. All happy. No guns. No fighting.'

Olivier hesitated. There was a part of him, an urgent, powerful part, that surged with anger, that wanted to shake this pathetic old man and shout at him, You killed these children, you mad fool. You haven't kept them safe! You've murdered them! But there was another part of him, the part that had made him such a great policeman for so many years, that needed more than anything to understand.

'Monsieur,' he began slowly. 'I'm not sure I understand. What do you mean again?'

Mathieu shivered more violently and began plucking at his clothes. 'Like Gilles, and Colin, and Jean-Jacques,' he muttered. 'They hated the war, hated it, the guns, the noise, the screams. They hated it and then they died.' He turned his anxious face to Olivier, 'You do see, don't you? I couldn't let it happen again. I had to keep them safe.'

'Please, monsieur, I don't want to upset you, but when did this happen? Where were those men killed?'

'Why at Sedan, of course.'

And suddenly it all fell into place.

The idiotic war that grandiose little man and his minions had started forty years and more before, rushing to attack the Germans. Eager and utterly unprepared.

'Again, forgive me, monsieur, I really don't want to hurt you, but how were you at Sedan? You must have been very young.'

'Oh yes, very young, and very foolish.' A sudden smile lit up his ravaged features for a moment. 'There were seven of us, all just out of school. We joined the Reserves, thinking we'd have more luck with the girls if we were in uniform. We had no intention of being soldiers. It never entered our heads. But then the war came, and the generals found that they hadn't done their sums properly, and they simply didn't have enough soldiers, and so they called up all the Reserves.

And that was that, there we are, soldiers. Gilles, Colin, André and Jean-Jacques were killed in the battle. Alain committed suicide a few months later, and Jean-Marie drank himself to death slowly, over the years.'

'And you became a schoolteacher.'

'Yes. I thought, idiot that I was, that if I could teach boys to think and care about the world and each other, then they would grow up into men who would not go to war.' A silence. 'It hasn't quite worked like that, has it?'

'You know you're going to have to come with me to the police station?'

'But I can't leave the children! I have to look after them.'

Olivier racked his brains. He didn't want to have to struggle with this desperately sick, broken-hearted, broken-minded old man.

'But you need to tell the gendarmes where the children are, and who they are, so that their families won't worry any more, don't you? Then you can come back and look after them all again.'

He held his breath, hoping the lie would work.

'Of course, of course. You're right. The families should know, however hopeless they are.' And Mathieu stood, almost impatiently holding his hand out so that he could pull Olivier to his feet. Together the two men walked through the wood and along the paths towards the distant village. They trudged in step, each deep in their own thoughts.

It was when they had almost reached the road that led down to the village that it happened.

The road was full of men and vehicles hurrying to the front, with a line of tanks pushing as fast as they could towards the fighting. Mathieu saw the crowd of soldiers, the urgent movements, the huge metal-plated machines hurtling to destroy and be destroyed. With a cry he rushed forward and tumbled in front of one of the tanks, landing on his knees, his arms outstretched as if to stop it. The tank driver saw nothing, and the tank drove on over the kneeling man, over and past, leaving the crushed body lying in a heap in the road.

Cries went up, the column halted, the tank driver climbed slowly out of his cab and walked slowly back to where Olivier was standing beside the body.

'I didn't see him, sir, I couldn't stop.' The soldier was distraught.

'It's not your fault, there was nothing you could do. Please, go back to your tank, and go where you are needed.'

A cavalry captain rode up at the head of a squadron of horse. He summed up the situation with a glance.

'Corporal, go back and rustle up some stretcher bearers, and then join us further up the road as quick as you can.'

The corporal saluted and rode off.

'Thank you, sir,' said Olivier.

'Can't wait with you, I'm afraid,' the captain said. 'Got Huns on the run up ahead. Don't want them all to get away before we've had our chance.' And he wheeled his horse round and led his troop away along the road.

Men and vans and tanks all started up again, leaving Olivier to wait with what was left of Mathieu Rivière, soldier, schoolmaster, child-killer.

Olivier stood, looking down at the broken body at his feet as he heard the rising clank and grind of the vehicles moving up to the front line.

So this is what victory looks like, he thought.

Epilogue

At first it seemed as though the battle of Cambrai had been a remarkable success for the allied forces. By November 30th, though, the Germans began a devastating counter-attack which regained much of the ground which had been overrun by the British in the early days of the battle, and which then swept even further forward. Civilians and soldiers alike fled from the swiftly advancing German forces near Gouzeaucourt. The little clearing in the wood, after a sudden flurry of frightened men running through it, settled back into silence, guarding the small bodies that were to lie there undisturbed for nearly a hundred years.

Acknowledgements

A novel is never the work of just one person, and this has been the fruit of many people's knowledge, expertise and patient understanding. I am enormously grateful to all those who have pointed me in the right direction, and to those who have put up with the episodes of moroseness and mania which make up a writer's life. Thank you particularly to Nicholas Marquez-Grant, a prince among forensic anthropologists, and to Katharine Shiel for her meticulous editing, and to all my forbearing family and friends, especially JAS.

Also from Crime Scene Books

The Richebourg Affair
By R.M.Cartmel

The first in a series following the acute if rumpled Inspector Truchaud of the French police as he pursues fraudsters, murderers and gangsters over the course of a winemaking year in the vineyards of Burgundy.

In *The Richebourg Affair,* Truchaud, an Inspector in the Paris police, finds himself summoned home to the family vineyard in Burgundy on the death of his older brother. His brother's wife is bereft, their son is bemused, and Truchaud's father is increasingly bewildered. What had seemed a simple private family tragedy soon turns into a criminal investigation, as Truchaud becomes embroiled in uncovering murder, fraud and a secret which has remained hidden since World War II.

"A well-crafted treasure of unforgettable characters." *Jeffrey Siger*

"A very complex mystery with lots of different elements. R.M. Cartmel was born to write." *Sharon Powell*

"I loved this book." *Laura Hartman*

"The characterisation is wonderfully well done. Everyone in this book felt alive." *rambles.net*

"R.M Cartmel joins the ranks of the best classic crime writers here:

one whose mystery has the full character development of any novel, with believable events, attention to police procedures - and that hard to define element which makes the story very difficult to put down. I rank R.M. Cartmel with my own personal favourite, Dame Ngaio Marsh, and am delighted to discover this contemporary writer creating mysteries. This one is right at the top of the charts!" *Long and Short Reviews*

The Charlemagne Connection
By R.M.Cartmel

The second in the Inspector Truchaud series finds the diffident policeman unravelling yet another mystery in the little Burgundy village of Nuits-Saint-Georges. A young German tourist seems to have gone missing. But what at first appears quite a straightforward affair soon turns dark when a decomposing body is found in the woods.

Another episode of murder, mayhem, violence and villainy in the orderly vineyards of Burgundy.

"Like the vineyards of Nuits-Saint-Georges, Cartmel is in fine form as he once again teams up with France's laconic and witty crime solver. Red herrings and shocks galore, interspersed with villainy, violence and vinification make The Charlemagne Connection a compulsive and highly satisfying intelligent read." *Sam Millar, New York Review of Books*

The Romanée Vintage
By R.M.Cartmel

In the third of R.M. Cartmel's 'wine and crime' thrillers featuring Inspector Truchaud, it seems that it is not only the grapes which ripened over the course of the hot Burgundy summer.

Vengeance hangs heavy in the air, with explosive results.

"This is an intelligent and well-researched story by a writer who clearly loves the wines and people of Burgundy. It is a Grand Cru of a novel that will delight both crime fans and oenophiles." *L.C. Tyler, award-winning author of the John Grey historical mysteries and the Ethelred and Elsie series*

"After an explosive start, RM Cartmel's latest vintage offering slips down very easily, with an intriguing finish." *Jasper Morris, Master of Wine, author of Inside Burgundy*

Captcha Thief
By Rosie Claverton

Agoraphobic hacker Amy Lane and her sidekick ex-con Jason Carr are caught in a tortuous and increasingly dangerous adventure as Amy seeks to help track an art thief and Jason seeks to impress the National Crime Agency investigator Frieda Haas sent to recover the missing painting - and its abductor.

As the evidence leads Amy and the police in circles, Jason finds himself taking more and more risks in his hunt for the thief. Nothing is as it seems. Are Amy and Jason merely playthings for a vicious murderer? Can they survive the game?

"I have to applaud Claverton for her resourcefulness to deftly handle labyrinthine plot twists as it moves in four different directions involving conflicts between Jason and Amy, Jason and Frieda, Amy alone and the crime's perpetrator, as well as her innovative manner in weaving geocaching into the plot that threw me for quite a loop. In addition, Claverton understands that mystery stories should not be simple or clean as we don't want to read stories that are easily resolved. Consequently, to engage our desperate need to know, she has crafted a story that evolves, evades and leaves pieces out with unanswered questions, riddles and confusion trapping us in the moment and compelling us to read on by its incompleteness. I have to admit that when reading any mystery or for that matter any novel, I enjoy working and bringing part of myself to the table in filling in the blanks which is exactly what Claverton has accomplished with *Captcha Thief.*" *Norm Goldman, BookPleasures.com*

"Deft writing, fabulous characterisation and a plot that never lets go." *Dave Sivers, author of the Archer and Baines crime series*

"Rosie Claverton has played the alchemist, and created literary gold." *Crime Fiction Lover*

"I am firmly hooked on the Amy and Jason chronicles." *Dear Author Recommended Read*

"Be prepared for a thrilling ride." *RT Magazine*

Terror 404
By Rosie Claverton

Terror 404 is the fourth in the Amy Lane mysteries series. Amy Lane, agoraphobic grey-hat hacker, has been isolated in a private psychiatric hospital, away from friends, associates and every form of connection to the web. Jason, her trusted companion and co-conspirator, is in hiding and on the run. When a fellow hospital patient is mysteriously murdered, Amy and Jason must find a way to join forces to solve the murder and save themselves.

"Rosie Claverton has produced a highly original heroine with truly authentic strengths and flaws, in this stunning addition to the psychological crime thriller genre. Definitely recommended."
Zoë Sharp, creator of the bestselling Charlie Fox series

50 Miles from Anywhere
By Michael Cayzer

It could never happen here - or could it? Ever wondered what really goes on in the place where you live? What did happen to that kid in your class who disappeared, never to be seen again? What is the story behind that nice little girl who works in the tea-shop? Which street should you nip down for your evening's supply of drugs? For that matter, just where did those drugs come from?

When these questions come bubbling to the surface of a seemingly quiet little English town, no-one's happy with the answers.

Michael Cayzer's new thriller chills from the very first page as it takes the reader on a desperate journey through failed lives, lost hopes and last chances.

"One of those books classed under 'can't put down', the plot rips the dark underbelly out of the provincial city. Woven with characters and sub-plots that perhaps realistically ring true of any city of its time which has become subject to mass migration. A modern thriller and crime story which without gore describes the violent brutality of gangs , corruption and exploitation. No one central character emerges but a subset of plausible would-be leads that rush in and fade out and reappear with nonchalance, but with effect."
Amazon reviewer

Dead Pretty
By Candy Denman

Dr Jocasta (Jo) Hughes, thirty two years old, a willowy blonde with a wicked sense of humour and an unsatisfactory love life, works part time as a GP in Hastings, a small English fishing town, and is on call as a Forensic Medical Practitioner for the local police. As it becomes clear that there is a serial killer on the loose in the town, Jo finds herself increasingly at risk.

"*Dead Pretty* is a wonderful mixture of the cosy and the creepy. The killer is repulsively nasty, and all too believable, while the heroine, Dr Jo Hughes, is a witty, sensible, silly woman it's a real pleasure to spend time with." *Amazon reviewer*

The Poison Cell
By Julain Hayes

The true story behind one of the shoddiest episodes of political intrigue and outright lies in the lead-up to the Iraq war. A seventeen-year-old boy asleep in his flat, the police pound at the door, a nightmare begins. Not Moscow under Stalin, but London 2003, in thebuild-up to the invasion of Iraq. A terrifying true story of power, pressure, and political perversion - and of the hard-won triumph of truth and integrity. Julian Hayes, the criminal defence lawyer who represented the teenaged Sidali, tells in vivid detail the nail-biting story of his arrest, trial, and eventual exoneration.

Julian is a hugely experienced lawyer, specialising in criminal law. This is his first book.

"This is the story of a process that was long and arduous but did, ultimately, demonstrate the true value of the jury system and why it should always underpin our criminal justice system." *Toby Hedworth QC*